Kiss Of Affliction

KRISTA MACBEATH

1st Edition

ISBN: 0993832202
ISBN-13: 978-0993832208

DEDICATION

To my readers, thank you so much for buying Kiss of Affliction. I can't wait to share the next installment of the Never Kissed series!

CONTENTS

ACKNOWLEDGMENTS

There is no way I could have written this book without the emotional and physical support of the closest people in my world. A meager thank you doesn't begin to express my gratitude for cheering me on to the finish line.
My husband, the patience that man has for my ideas and dreams. At every angle, he made this happen. He's been the perfect support that I needed to be able to call myself an author, mom, and wife. I will always put my family first, but he never made me chose between writing and being all I can be for my family.

Whatever you see in me makes me want to see it in myself. I love you so much for giving me this opportunity and to prove to our children they can dream as big as the stars. You have my meager thanks and my heart.

To my nine year old son, Brayden, who gives me space when I need to write, and love when he can see it's been a hard day being creative. Who took it upon himself to learn how to use my Keurig, and knows exactly how I take my coffee. To my eight year old daughter, Keyra, who can make me laugh in any moment. Who wrote a book in her class ' like mommy', which made me beam with pride. She'd let me borrow her headphones because she knows how I consider my writing playlist a part of my creative process. These small moments have made me a better mom, and a focused writer. I love you both with my every breath.

My parents, who were never rich but always gave me a home to come back to. Thanks for putting up with me all these years. I'll be over this weekend, what's for supper? ;)

A huge part of my writing process is my best friend, my master beta, my sister in so many ways. Robyn, we both know this book wouldn't have lifted a page past chapter three if it wasn't for you. For all the times I stopped lacking inspiration or energy. For all the times you slapped my hand for editing too much. For not only being the first one to read everything I write, but for wanting to. Your honesty has been worth more than any currency, this book is for you. You mean so much to me, you inspire me to push harder, higher, and to expect things in myself I never thought I should. You are so busy, but you always find time for me and this book. Here's to many more stories, many more books, and many more days as besties!

Lastly, as I mentioned, the music I listened to guided me through many of the emotions I had to breach to get this story written. Emotions I've known all too well, but the music were the key to open the door and allow me to explore the inner mind of these emotions. Some days it wasn't easy to go there mentally, but these artists helped make it happen and I hold their lyrics and music dear to my heart. I just want to personally thank a few, and I highly suggest you buy their albums! Andy Brown, James Arthur, Serena Ryder, Sister Hazel, Jenn Grant, and definitely not the least, The Civil Wars. I adore their originals, but an acoustic version always rubs me in all the right ways.

Thanks to you, my readers, every single purchase encourages me to go forward.

CHAPTER 1

All apologies have been said. All comforts have been lost, on me. I am no one. No one ready to give an ounce of color to any taker who tries. Pitied looks are cast my way. I am in my best black dress, which is my only dress. I feel like all my blood has drained out the bottom of my feet. So, I sit with numbness as my only emotion. Frozen in this moment.

"You should eat something."

I faintly heard a voice over my clouded thoughts. There is a hand on my shoulder, but it doesn't register as me being touched. My body rejects any warmth coming from anything. All I can do is sit here, mechanically, looking out at the sea of black flowing by me.

I want to leave, I want to run far from here.

That distant voice is speaking to me again, I can barely make out what he is saying over the numbing noise echoing inside my head. Like static on a television, and there is nothing in me to fight it off.

Dragging my eyes up to the body now in front of me, I stopped on a concerned pair of eyes. Unusually dressed in a coordinating black suit, white dress shirt, and a deep red skinny tie. Kneeling down in front of me, I slowly registered Max's presence. Realizing the warmth sliding down from my shoulder came from his hand still holding me there.

His voice soft, washed over me, "Vi? Can I get you some coffee or food?"

I've known Max since elementary school. It's a small town and it's hard not to know everyone, even those you don't want to know. Before grade four I had seen him around the school, the quiet kid who kept to himself. The first day of fourth grade he and my brother, Alex, were seated right behind me. They struck up a tight friendship, and everything naturally fell into place between them, and solidified a bond between us three.

Alex was supposed to go onto grade five that year, but failed. So he was held back a grade, my grade, and in my class. We were typical siblings as kids, but I always considered myself pretty lucky. Maybe that wasn't so typical as a sister. Once we were teenagers, they always invited me to hang out with them. Looking back, I know that it wasn't just that I was his sister, all three of us were friends. It seems like it was always just the three of us. I never felt the need to have best friends like the other girls my age. I could always count on them to be around, so I never tried to fit in anywhere. They were all I wanted.

Things changed in high school. We still hung out, but if the chance was there, they were hanging out with their group of friends. Max and Alex were the typical teenage guys. They enjoyed partying and driving around at all hours, with their music blocking out any form of logical thinking. I was always the kid sister. Not that this stopped them from trying to get me to go with them. I only took them up on their offer twice. They were super social, and I wasn't. Fitting in with their friends didn't come naturally to me, I'd much rather stay home to read and get lost in a fictional world. Max always stayed by my side though, he was like my adopted big brother. He and Alex would always be there for me, even if their protective big brother status was really annoying some times.

Max reminded me of Alex. Tall, broad across the shoulders, messy hair which makes the natural nonchalant style look pulled together. Always in jeans, t-shirt, and sneakers, never feeling the need to blend in with the high society types and typical athletes that Black River attracts.

My brother, Alex.

The blanket of darkness with the thought of his name started covering over me again. Retreating into myself is the only way I know how to get through this. If this Church were on fire I wouldn't be able to run, I am anchored here, paralyzed, unable to move.

"Vi, you aren't looking well, you're really pale. Vi? You listening to me?" Max was speaking calmly, but I could hear the slightest thread of angst in his voice. That pulled my thoughts back to his face. Max doesn't do panic, he has always been calm and collected.

"What are you talking about Max? I can barely move my body, I feel so…numb. Food is honestly the last thing I want."

"Maybe I should take you to the hospital to get checked out." His hand moved from my shoulder to rub the back of his neck while his train of thought led him further down that rabbit hole.

I shot a glance to him, only allowing myself to feel one emotion at a time, and he read it on my face.

"You know I'm not going back there." My tone more cold than I should ever allow towards him.

He stayed in front of me, rubbing my bare arms, trying to get my body to come back to life.

I sluggishly turned my eyes back to the room which was starting to slowly thin out. Refreshments have been had, condolences have been made, and they get to go back to their regular lives and schedules.

Max's warm hand rested once again on my shoulder while he stood and walked around to stand behind me. It was giving me the only warm sensation in my hollow body. I reached up and grabbed it, my cold fingers couldn't let go. I felt like the fog in the room, everybody was trying to look through me. Max didn't have to.

Soon the room was empty. The caterers were clearing the tables and trying hard not to look my way, like I was the plague. The sun was starting to shine through the basement windows of the reception room. I vaguely scanned the emptiness of the room and saw Pastor Cauley was making his way over to me. Dressed in his black suit, with his side swept white hair shining in the patch of sunlight coming through the stained glass window. The Pastor has known me since the day I was born, it was hard to see the look of concern on his face.

It took every bit of will in me to make my body do its duty, and stand. Once up, my knees started to be unresponsive, beginning to buckle, refusing the movement I was forcing.

Stubbornly, I wouldn't let them. This was my responsibility, and I couldn't let my family down.

He cupped his warm hands around my ice cold ones with a gentleness that should have truly touched me. But, it is impossible for me to feel anything. Vacant, I looked at him.

He paused struggling for words, and gently sighed, his shoulders giving way to the emotions of the day.

His gentle dark eyes trying to read my soul, "Everything is done and I've looked after the burial arrangements. The hearse is on its way to the cemetery."

Pausing to collect his words, he gave me what he hoped were comforting words.

"This is certainly a tragedy. May God give you strength in this difficult time. The Church is always here for you Violet."

My knees, my knees are going to give out any minute. Max took a step from behind me and put his arm around my waist to give me the support my body and heart needed. The sobs leaching themselves out of my throat sounded unlike me, and surprised the catering staff. A coffee cup smashed to the floor making me jump.

Frantically I tried to focus on something to relieve me of my thoughts. My eyes landed on a coffee stain near my feet that the carpet provided. Any focus, anything was better than the topic of this conversation. I pleaded with myself for the tears brimming in my eyes to recede. I really don't want to talk about this.

"Are you sure you can get home safely? Is there anybody staying with you tonight?" Pastor Cauley asked softly, his words saturated with anguish, his hands tightened in worry over mine.

Max cleared his throat, his voice cracking with his own sorrow, "I'm bringing her home and will be staying with her for as long as she needs."

Giving me a squeeze with his arm at my waist, I looked up from the carpet to really see Max for the first time in days. The twisted emotions haunting his face, reflecting my own. What strength he had was fading, he looked more tired than I had ever seen him. His face was set like stone, a feeling I understood. He was fighting for strength, and giving it all to me.

Natural instinct made me turn in to him taking my hands slowly from the priest's, and wrapping them around Max. He knew, even if not in it's entirety, how much I needed him. Only with him could I find myself, and he let me surrender to that dismal truth. Tears ran down my face staining his jacket and tie. The sobs returning, while I heard myself through gasps of air saying, "They're gone."

His arms held me up, resting his cheek on the top of my head. One hand rubbing my back in slight, smooth strokes. I could feel his sharp intakes of breath while he silently cried with me.

I knew at that point that I may have lost everything, my family, my best friend, my life, but I still had Max. A shred of something that once was.

Max spoke quietly with the pastor as I walked over to

gather my coat and purse. A middle aged woman in her catering uniform was finishing up the last table with its dirty dishes.

"Thank you." I said to her in a very hoarse voice. She smiled a tortured smile.

"You are welcome, and I'm so sorry for your loss."

I gave her the slightest of a smile, everything I could pull to my face as a thank you. Then turned and put on my coat, and thought, 'So am I'.

Walking out to the parking lot, the cool early summer's breeze drugged some of my haze. Finally giving me a subtle break from my constant numbness.

I walked around the brick building, Max's protective arm still around my waist.

The new black S.U.V. was the only vehicle sitting in the parking lot. Max's father gave it to him as an early graduation present. His parents divorced a couple years after we became friends. They enjoy over compensating for their short comings in parenting by spoiling their only son.

The drive on the old country road was quiet. Neither one of us had anything to say. The quiet emptiness suited us. Nothing could be said that would make us feel any better. We live with our numbed disbelief that is the present, and completely possesses us.

The shadow of an old song lurked up the back of my mind. The more attention I gave it, the more it took over my thoughts until I was able to place what it was and where I had heard it.

The family would spend our summer vacation at Gram's country home. It was a typical big country house with fields all around. Beautiful, natural, and to me, magical. She'd sing us an old song her Grandmother used to sing to her, usually while we walked around outside or picked vegetables from her garden.

A memory framed in my mind was of the last visit we made before she had a stroke and died shortly after. Alex and I were in the living room thinking we were professional pianists, banging on the out of tune piano, repeating each other's musical patterns. Me in the high key, Alex in the low. It drove our parents crazy.

Dad would always say, "That hasn't been tuned since Dad tuned it last."

Around that time, Grampy would have been gone for a few years. I could remember the smell of his pipe, but I was too young to have really vivid memories of him.

I never knew if Dad was joking or not. I didn't know what an out of tune key sounded like compared to a tuned one. The antique piano always sounded this way, and Alex and I were obviously pros.

Gram came in and asked us if we'd like to go for a walk out in the fields behind her house, which was full of wild daisies. The field stretched uphill until it met the horizon. The vast space was lined with trees and bushes giving many homes to many creatures. She hummed a tune while holding my hand, walking up the path to the skyline. The sun was golden on her white hair. As I looked up at her, she looked down at me with a gentle smile. I felt her squeeze my hand while never breaking her song. Then her gaze shifted up to Alex who was ahead of us trying to catch a grasshopper. It was a perfect moment. A moment of happiness capsuled in my mind.

Now she and Gramps are gone, Mom and Dad are gone, and Alex too. I am all that is left in our family.

I was staring out the window in a zombie state, completely buried in the memories. I'm constantly pulled back to this awful dream and I can't wake myself up. The drive was so quiet that I kept going deeper and darker with the certainty of my fate. However long the drive, I only pulled back to consciousness when the gear shift was put in park, and the sound of the emergency brake being engaged between our seats broke it completely.

KISS OF AFFLICTION

CHAPTER 2

We sat in front of my parent's oversized Cape Cod style house. It was draped in darkness. The sun had finally surrendered to what is officially the worst few days in my 19 years. Streaks of its pinkish leftovers from the day hung in the sky, giving me enough light to see the outline of my vacant home.

I felt Max's eyes on me. It was dark around us, but I could see him looking. I wondered what he must see right now. We stared at each other waiting for the other to break the silence. Neither one of us wanted to face the house. Max had been here so many times escaping the drama sparking over at his parent's houses, that this was Max's second home. Finally he was the one to break the lull.

"We have to do this sooner or later."

Slowly, his body obviously tired, he unbuckled his seatbelt and opened the door. I could feel the cold night air slapping me in the face. I started gathering the black trench coat that my Mother had given me this past

Christmas. She thought it was a great idea to give me something that was beyond my sweaters and jeans. I doubt she had in mind that its first use would be to her funeral. I froze with the realization that last Christmas will be my last with my Mother, and my family. The crushing weight was back in my head, sinking further down to my chest, making it difficult to breathe.

My door opened and the cold air slapped me again. Unfortunately, snapping me right back into my spiraling reality. Being tossed mentally from one memory to another, then back to the present was far from a reprieve.

Slowly walking around Max's Jeep, to the cobblestone walkway, I couldn't help but look down. Along the path to the front door were the flowers my mother had just planted. The earth was still loose around the bare looking pink buds, waiting for my Mother's green thumb to take care of them.

Reaching the front steps, I slowed to nearly a stop. Hanging my head down, my body so tense it couldn't move in any other way. I couldn't make the first step up the stairs. Stepping up to a fate I didn't want, I didn't ask for, wasn't something I was willing to do voluntarily. I couldn't accept any of this. THIS is not how I wanted to live my life. I wanted my Mother to be here when I had questions about women things. I wanted my Father to walk me down the aisle if I ever decided to get married. I need my brother to make me see the reality of my stupid meaningless situations and to tell me that not everything can be as dreamy like characters in a novel. I can't live without them. I can barely breathe without them.

I looked up, past the door, and my eyes landed on the window a few feet above it. My terror finally started seeping into my outside world. I was staring into Alex's bedroom window. It's the middle upper window, peeking out from the roof. I know beyond the glass lays an emptiness, one that is my very own.

Suddenly Max's arm was again around my waist, pulling me out of a slow understanding of how empty my house truly is. Was this really home now? Without them? I was unaware I was already moving up the stairs nearing the front door, before I even realized I was there. Max knew the key was hidden under the plant stand on the front porch, I am sure he has used it many times to sneak Alex home after a long night out.

He opened the door, and again, it took everything in me just to stand, let alone to take the step forward that I knew was more than the physical action. It was towards something I couldn't accept. Everything was dark inside, mirroring me.

"Should I go inside and turn on some lights?"

Again, his words were distant and clouded. I could barely make out what he asked, he had spoken so low.

Max knew the question was a rhetorical one. My empty stare gave him enough of an answer I guess, my heart frozen with my body. Crossing the threshold makes this dreadful illusion a reality. It means I accept the circumstances, and I don't. Everything happened so fast. I'm not ready to move forward, to live alone, to begin where there was no end to the end.

The soft glow from the lamp lit up the beginning of what was now my solitude. I tried to focus inside the entry way on Max standing there, looking back at me expecting nothing at all. What he sees isn't the friend he once knew.

No words needed to be spoken between he and I. Max walked toward me holding out his hand. I took it and stepped into a house I no longer felt was my home.

I walked through the foyer, to the staircase.

"Max?"

His name barely made a sound past my lips. My back was to him while I sluggishly slung my jacket and purse on the stair case.

Max sat down on the bench in the hall, wearily taking off his dress shoes.

He paused to look at me, "Yeah?"

I turned my body to face him, "Thank you."

My eyes caught his, and he looked at me with an intense depth that almost frightened me. It made something inside me shift knowing that he was in pain.

"For the last couple of days, and for not leaving me alone tonight." I wanted to break away from his burning gaze. My eyes were locked to his, both of us were gripping to whatever we had left.

I hadn't noticed how worn he looked until now. I mean, I knew he was exhausted, and the sadness of everything dug deep into him. The soft light from the lamp enhanced the lines on his weathered face. He didn't take his eyes from mine as I took three steps toward him. I could see pieces of myself in his eyes. I sat down on the bench next to him and reciprocated the moments when he held me. His arms didn't hesitate and his hug felt anxious and needy. It felt good to hold him this time. It was nice to be needed, it gave me a purpose other than pushing myself for my next breath.

Our hug lasted for what seemed like a long time. The grandfather clock ticked loudly with each second. Time wouldn't stand still. We needed that connection to know that we weren't alone. The way Max hugged me back spoke volumes. He was never the type to spill his emotions. I always had to pry his problems out of him. I have an innate ability to tell when there was something wrong with him. He'd always say I am the only person who really got him. I figured that is what happened in time, you got to know somebody inside and out. After all this time, we knew each other better than we knew ourselves.

Pulling back I took in Max's tear stained face. My palm gently met his cheek, and I carefully wiped his tears away with my thumb, trying to rid him of the ache that I felt as well. He had been so strong for me these past four days. Something in me knew I wouldn't be able to give it all back to him, which I knew made me a bad friend. He deserved at least that. For tonight, I would give him what little I had.

My eyes left his, "Max, I haven't been very thoughtful these last few days. I really appreciate you sticking by me through all of this."

On my last spoken word, I looked back up to his gaze, and couldn't stop the tears from falling from my eyes once more.

Max pulled me back in to him, "What do you need Vi? If I don't have something to focus on I feel like I'm going out of my mind, so please just give me something to do. I want to take care of you, just tell me what you want."

"I don't know, I just need something to make me forget this emptiness. I need a break from it for a bit." Hot tears and frustration towards myself crept into my last few words.

I took myself from his hold and turned to lean back against the wall beside him.

My thoughts kept coming out loud.

"I can't keep feeling like this, the pain, it's too much! I hate it!"

Max shifted on the bench and got up to stand right in front of me. I looked up, a little taken aback by his fast movements in the middle of my venting. His face was hard and I noticed my words had made him cry. Again.

I took his hands in mine, "I'm so sorry Max. I didn't mean to make this harder for you, tell me what you need, and I will try…"

I knew there was nothing I could do for him. Just like there was nothing he could do for me. Our lives were never going to be what they once were.

Instinctively, I stood up with the idea of doing something right now was better than nothing. I almost fell back down to the bench because of Max's closeness, but threw my arms around his neck at the same time his hands held the small of my back to give me balance. He held me tight, wrapping himself around me, and we cried together once more. The more I cried, the harder the ache in my chest pained. I couldn't reverse the never ending cycle.

Max's arms were the only thing keeping me together,

so I wouldn't give in to the feeling of caving in on myself. His other hand started stroking my hair, and I realized he had stopped crying. Agitated with my sobs, my tears, and my neediness, I lessened my hold on him and slowly tried to back away. I could feel my anger engulfing the sadness and I wanted to run, or punch, or kick anything.

"God Max, why do you want to stay around me? I'm a mess! I'm seriously an awful friend." I didn't dare suggest he leave to have a better evening than what I knew I was about to have. I needed him here with me. I knew I wouldn't let him go if he agreed to it, but I wished I was that strong.

Max's arm tensed around my waist just as he was about to let go. The jerkiness of my withdrawal triggered him to react just as quickly, and he pulled his head back to look at my face. I glanced up while wiping at my face with the palm of my hand. His face was back to being hard, as if I made him unhappy. The voice in my head scoffed at how bad of a friend I obviously was.

In a quick gesture, he hooked his arm under my bare legs and scooped me up. Without any words, he started walking towards the kitchen. I wasn't sure if it was the shock or my anxiety of actually walking around this haunted house, but anger was taking over as my only emotion.

"Max, put me down! I don't want to go anywhere in this house. Please, just put me down, I want to leave."

He brought me through the kitchen, to the back door, heading out of the house into the back yard.

"Vi, let's get one thing clear, you are not a bad friend, if you were I wouldn't be here. And I don't want to be in that house any more than you do, but eventually we will both have to face it. You can be mad at me, I don't care, but I'm not letting you go, not tonight, not ever. Deal with it."

If I could cry any more, I would have. I gave in to the fight, and slumped into his body, taking the comfort he was giving me. Every step he took, the anger melted away.

"I may not be a bad friend, but I'm not a good one neither." I mumbled as I let my head rest on his shoulder.

In the backyard, there was a pathway lit with solar lights. Max followed the very familiar pathway, and I knew exactly where we were going. Dad had built the screened in gazebo for Mom for their 25th anniversary. The stone fireplace was supposed to resemble the one they had at their Italian villa while on their honeymoon.

This was our haven though, I guess we sort of took it over as we got older and needed a place beyond the walls of the living room. It was where homework was done, where Alex played his guitar, where we ate our meals, where we'd just hang out. Where I'd always go to read.

There was a still and comforting silence that rested between Max and I as he set me down on the wicker sofa. I grabbed his hand before he pulled it away from me.

"I'm not mad at you Max." My throat cracking with the effort to talk low.

He leaned in and kissed my forehead and whispered, "I know."

He grabbed the old abused quilt that was hung on the back of the sofa and wrapped me in it.

We didn't need to be something for one another, I realized. It was alright to just be how we felt, together.

Max immediately started a fire with the wood my Father would have split and piled in the corner only a few days ago. The fire flickered and started catching right away, shedding some light in our sanctuary.

In the corner of my eye I caught the sheen off of Alex's guitar. It was sitting on the coffee table, which would have been from the last time he would have played it. The green pick shoved in between the strings.

Max had the fire crackling and snapping, and it was starting to throw some heat my way. He came over and sat down, wrapping his arms around me rubbing over the blanket to keep me warm.

"Are you warm enough?"

I nodded, gazing into the fire. His fingers found my knuckles where I was holding the blanket, and he mindlessly brushed me back and forth there.

"Why don't you try and get some sleep." Max said, pulling his attention to my face.

I shook my head, still looking into the fire.

"I can't, I only dream of them. They become too real."

After a few moments of quiet, Max let go of his hold on me. He leaned over, and picked up Alex's guitar. Going to the other end of the sofa, he pulled a pillow from behind him and leaned it against the side of his leg.

He patted it, "Lay down, I will stay up and keep an eye on you. If you are restless or scream in your sleep like last night, I will wake you up, ok?"

I knew there was nothing he could do about my dreams, but the warmth from the fire was starting to make my eyes heavy. I stretched out and rested my head on the pillow, and kept my eyes on the fire while it danced under the stone hearth.

Max plucked a few chords on the guitar, letting his fingers figure out what song to play. They fumbled around searching for the proper chords. The variations ebbed, into a tune I recognized. Max naturally strummed Black Bird by the Beatles which Alex would play for me every time there was chaos in my life. Annoyingly so. He'd strum the mellow tune even in the midst of an argument. I guess he'd play it to calm me down and shut me up. He knew it'd frustrate me. When I'm mad, I want to be mad, not placated by a mellow song to avoid the issue. The outcome would always be me throwing a pillow at his face. I hated that it always worked, even though he drove me insane and never wanted to engage in my arguments. It was just his way of chilling me out from any drama.

After Max fingered the first few chords, he started singing the lyrics. His low, barely audible, voice hummed it at first. Then the words started forming as the song continued. I slowly moved my gaze upwards to see past the guitar.

His reflection looked like glass, with the reflection of the fire. His eyes closed, he was transported somewhere else. I had never heard Max sing before, he'd always accompany Alex with his guitar, but Alex always did the singing. I barely breathed, I didn't want to break the trance he was in. I hated that I found it beautiful.

I knew then that this was Max's goodbye to my brother. To our brother. We were honouring him with my song. Regardless if I was ready, it had been four days and I hadn't said goodbye or let him go. Not in the way that Alex would hear it. Not in my soul. I didn't want to leave my brother, not once had he ever left me. Until now.

On the last verse, tears swam from my eyes freely, down each of my cheeks to the pillow. I was stone, like a statue except for the tears that were constantly flowing. 'Bye Alex' a whisper crept up the back of my mind, without warning. I closed my eyes in the silence of the last note. It can't be over. I begged the universe to reverse time. Max's arms were around me at once, at the same time mine searched out for him. We cried the hardest we had ever during this whole dismal situation.

I fell asleep on Max's chest, crying myself into unconsciousness. With the words playing over and over in my head.

"Bye Alex."

CHAPTER 3

"I will instruct my sorrows to be proud,
For grief is proud and makes his owner stoop.
To me and to the state of my great grief
Let kings assemble, for my grief's so great
That no supporter but the huge firm earth
Can hold it up."

--William Shakespeare

Slowly, I decided to open my eyes. I knew before accepting a new day that it was raining out. I could hear the patter of falling drops on the roof of the gazebo. The sweet rain air was fresh, but chilled. Heat from the fireplace allowed me to find some comfort, but the dampness crept into my bones regardless.

I realized that at some point between my last nightmare and now, Max had disappeared. Sitting up, I scanned the back yard trying to catch his silhouette within the thick coastal fog. The backdrop of the surrounding woods mixed with the haze offered little help of his whereabouts. I assumed he was inside the house, or possibly even left. Maybe he needed a break from me. It was a tough night, and I didn't make things any better by reacting the way I did, the way I always do. A break from me would do him some good. I haven't been the easiest to be around, and I'm starting to believe that is the way it will be for me every day from now on. My nightmares were intense, and I remember waking myself screaming with tears streaming down my face. Max's arms instantly tightened around me as soon as I woke, and I held onto him until my tears let me fall back under back into the reality of the dreams.

I gave up caring what time of day it was. Day is day, night is night. Time holds little value any more. Finding a moment to think everything over was very hard. I've had to be everyone's puppet, while being smothered with unwanted affection and attention. I robotically went along, feeling suffocated, turning inward.

Laying back down, I let my mind travel to where it wanted. Allowing myself to digest fragments of what has happened, and giving myself permission to remember.

I thought about Alex, and wondered if we were born as twins, would it hurt any worse with his loss. Could my pain possibly feel any more debilitating and gut wrenching.

We'd get the twin question a lot after Alex came in to my class. We definitely looked like siblings, but Max says it's in our mannerisms that make people wonder. We inherited Dad's green eyes and wavy dark brown hair. Unlike Alex's, mine is long. Most days I don't have patience for it, so it gets twisted and put on top of my head in a messy 'wherever it lands is fine by me' bun. Because, honestly, I just don't care.

Alex kept his hair meticulously long enough so there was some length turning out from under his worn out cap. Mom always insisted he not wear the hat so much so he could show off our "father's gift to women". Those words from Mom's mouth always made us cringe. I never understood going to the hairdresser's and explaining what should just be called the ball cap special. When he'd annoy me, I'd threaten to shave it in his sleep. I'd always tease him, "But I wouldn't want to see my big brother wake up and start crying over hair."

Through Mom's Irish DNA, we were graced with her slender sharp nose and sculpted soft curved lips. I always found it interesting how Alex and I seem to have been genetically given the same features, I guess I'm glad they were the good ones.
The only things not given to us by our parents were their height. I had already surpassed Mom's height of her petite frame. Alex always reminded me that I will always be shorter than him. Which I can honestly say, isn't a problem since he was six feet two inches. My five feet, six, suits me just fine.

He never was one to sit still, so he was built and muscular. Not by being in sports, but just from working in the garage and building things. I'm not built, not in a super skinny athletic trimmed body kind of way, but I can outrun Alex in a heartbeat. I love to run, to push my body just to feel my muscles burn.

I've been in Aikido for a couple years as well, which has given me back the confidence and freedom I thought I had lost. It also keeps me fit, so I am able to enjoy the relationship I have with gummy candies, it's the only thing I feel like eating when I'm reading. Once I get absorbed in a book, which is often, I become enraptured with the fictional characters, and I just don't want to think of anything else. Like a lost meal or two. It drove Mom nuts.

Unfortunately, my social life is pretty tame. My life is far from exciting intrigue and swept up romances. I have a few close friends at school, but I'm not one to do the girly thing, or feel the need to socialize much. I don't really fit in anywhere, but I'm also completely fine with that.

The date of my final exam was June 15th. Five days ago, I saw my brother sitting in the papasan chair across from me now. He was eating the pizza Mom had picked up on her way home from the office. My parents were busying themselves to attend a charity dinner at The Boat Club. Since our kitchen talents were limited to KD, she knew we'd go hungry without her motherly ability to see into the future and predict what would happen.

Alex was strumming a song when she delivered our plates of food to the gazebo. I can't think of what song it was now. Funny how those little details that never mattered before, matter so much once they are gone.

I was in this same uncomfortable rattan sofa, reading Mansfield Park by Jane Austen, again. My tattered, go to novel.

"Hey little sis, when are ya going to read something good? You know you can borrow any of my Stephen Gunn novels any time."

With a crooked smirk he sat his guitar down on the coffee table and shoved the pick between the strings on the neck. Shoveling down his dinner so fast, I'm sure he couldn't even taste it. Typical when he was cutting time short on a night out.

"Alex…chew! I don't know why Mom always orders

what you like on the pizza, you never take the time to taste it anyways."

As usual, my statement didn't get any reaction. He was too focused on getting out of the house, with his plans forming in his head. Selective hearing was a talent of his. I rolled my eyes.

Mom's rule was that we had to have a family supper at home before going out with our friends. This didn't prove to be a problem for me. I rarely went anywhere. The fact that I didn't have a car, unlike my brother, seemed to impede on that part of my social life.

"Where are you off to tonight?" I asked him after putting a ripped piece of paper to mark my spot in the book and grabbed my plate.

I had overheard conversations about a party tonight, and a few acquaintances had invited me as well. It was a Grad party at the deserted army base. Really, it was just a clearing in the woods everyone called the army base, which made it perfect for teenagers to pitch their tents, have a camp fire, and do what they normally do. Which, I'm sure, didn't involve singing camp songs. Alex and Max would be full of stories the Sunday after such parties about how wasted everyone got and what stupid things they did. I had already guessed that the guys were going to the party tonight.

"Hello...Alex...?"

"Uhh...There is a party back at the brook by the old army base. A bunch of us are bringing tents and spending the night. Finally being able to get out of this town once we graduate is something to celebrate! You should really come. I mean, I totally get why you don't normally come out with us, but nothing's going to happen Vi, you've got me and Max there."

Setting his plate down, he wadded up his unused napkin, and threw it in fireplace to await the next time it gets lit.

"Vi, you need to celebrate our upcoming freedom! Come out with us."

"If I didn't already have plans I'd actually, probably go. If only to shut you up."

I threw an innocent smirk his way. I knew he wouldn't be expecting my answer.

His emerald eyes set on me with interest. He was so protective over me, for good reason. I knew the Alexander the Great interrogation was about to start, big brother style.

"Where are you going?" He said, his full, stern attention on me now.

"Alex, I don't stay home because I'm afraid to go out. When I got out it's because I want to, not because that's all there is to do. I'm going to a movie tonight. I was hoping you'd give me a drive." I played my pleading innocent face with as much conviction to dissuade him from the next question, which was inevitably coming.

"I was talking to Kendra earlier, I know she and a few of your friends are going to the party. Who are you going to a movie with?"

My best friend, Kendra, knew full well what I was doing tonight. She obviously didn't tell Alex. I'm sure she knew how he'd react. She was one, of a very few, who knew what had happened to me two years ago.

"I'm going to meet Billy." I looked at him, half annoyed and part understanding why he wouldn't like the idea.

"Billy West? Football Billy? Oh my God Vi!" he snarled with disgust.

I couldn't help but laugh through my annoyance. Billy wasn't exactly my type, even if I don't know what my type is. He was extremely into sports and very well groomed and styled. Not that I didn't like a straight cut guy, but I think starving artist was generally my weakness.

We always joked about Billy. He came off pretty thick headed and arrogant. The type of arrogance that is hot, but can be a turn off too. His only thoughts were usually his game with girls, and the actual game he played on the school teams.

"Yes, Alex. Billy West." I sighed, leaning back against the back rest of the sofa, deflating at the idea of where this conversation was headed.

"He has been asking me for a while to go out with him. Persistence paid off, I guess."

The twisted face on Alex had me half mad. I was trying to be upset at his disdain for my choice of date. He can't stand Billy but he also doesn't know him. He just assumes that Billy only knows about football and is lacking in character for that reason. Maybe he is right, but I figure I have nothing to lose by giving Billy a little attention.

Getting impatient with him and his tortured faces, I

let out a sigh and stood up.

"It's not like I get asked out on a date often Alex! You scare every guy off before they can ask me! I love you and all, but the 'touch my little sister and I break your legs' routine is getting old. I needed your protection at one time, but I don't need it now."

I sighed, and softened my voice. "I get why you do it Alex. What happened with Skyler was messed up, but he isn't every guy. I'm glad you were there for me that night, but what have I been taking self-defense classes for? We both know I could kick your ass, that's good enough isn't it?" I tried to lightly joke. Even though me being pinned to the back seat of a car for my first time, with the idea of my body being at Skyler's, and his buddies disposal , wasn't exactly something I should joke about.

I was very lucky to have Alex and Max sneaking up to check on me since it was my first date. By the time they walked up the side road leading to the camping field everyone parties at, one guy was holding my arms while he stood at the passenger back door, while Skyler was trying to grab my feet at the other open door to hold them down. The dress I had meticulously planned out with Kendra that day became a horrible way of easy access. That's when Alex and Max completely lost it and took four guys on. It may have been out matched in numbers, but I knew all they saw was red. That day made us three much closer, and the guys were always over protective of me from that day on.

"Alex, I'm fine, and I will be fine. If I had to, I could handle things myself now. No guy will ever be worthy enough in your eyes, and I love you for it. But I need to be the one to make that call."

Alex sat pensive for a moment, then slowly stood up, a decision hardening on his face.

"But Vi, come on! Billy West! You can do better than that! Date anybody and you'd be doing better than him!"

I got tired of defending Billy. I agreed with Alex, but a date is a date, and I can't keep myself out of the dating game just because one went bad, really bad. Plus, it's not like my mind doesn't automatically go to that night a couple of years ago. I'm better prepared now, I can handle an attack from a guy double my size, or make him fall to his knees with one pressure point. I am the one in control, without it I would be completely lost.

I picked up the red and black floral pillow sitting on the sofa, and threw it at Alex. After a moment of catching him off guard, and my alter ego very happy with herself, I regained my composure. I still needed a drive to the movie theater.

"Alex, I really need a ride. Mom and Dad have plans, so I can't use the S.U.V., and I don't want to wait around after everyone here has left for Billy to show up."

Inwards, I cringed. I hated asking Alex for a ride. Getting him to drop me off gave him a physical presence and I knew if he saw Billy, an awkward, macho, big brother confrontation would most likely present itself. But I also didn't want Billy to pick me up, just something about him. I've just chalked it up to not knowing him or my overly cautious mind, but I still don't want to be alone with him in my house. Alex's thoughts on Billy's character, or lack of, isn't something I'd like to confirm while I'm home alone.

Alex drawls, with a slowly forming evil grin, "Sure..."

My alter ego deflates and face palms with a 'Why me?' expression on her face.

I sit in the uncomfortable passenger seat of my brother's hand me down 1972 muscle car driving along the highway. This royal blue beast has been in our family before it was one. It was Dad's car, and I'm sure it has seen better days, but it is Alex's pride and joy now. It was always a known fact in our family that he'd get the old car once he got his license. The heirloom wasn't one I wished for, so I was fine with how Alex and Dad spent endless hours working on it. I wouldn't know what to do if this thing stalled on the side of the road. Which it did. Frequently.

Alex carefully drove around the mall, to the back where the theatre was buzzing with many people from school. He pulled up to the movie theatre entrance with an eager expression, scanning the entrance of the Mall before putting the beast into park at the curb. I knew he was looking for Billy.

"Thanks for the ride. I guess I will see ya in the morning? Behave, and don't do anything stupid like last time!" I gave him a crooked smile.

A couple of weeks ago he was at one of his friend's birthday party, and was the first one in the pool. Naked. It was all I heard about at school, all the girls swooning over his bravado. It took all of my energy to block any mental pictures of that story.

I turned and tried to open the door in the process of saying my goodbye. I pulled relentlessly, exasperated at how nothing ever works on this car. Frustrated, and irritated, I scowled at him. I just wanted to get out before Billy showed up.

"Seriously Alex, is this some sort of master trick of yours to keep chicks in your car? I can't open the damn door!"

Alex, with an arrogant grin and a cocked eyebrow, reached across me and popped the metal lock up on the door.

"For starters, I don't need tricks to keep the ladies in the car, I'm more than enough for them to want to stay. Second, learn how to unlock a door before blaming old blue. You are insulting us both."

I couldn't keep my smile off my face. I punched him in the arm and chastised him the way a sister does to a brother, "Well if it had electric locks. Whatever, shut up." I smiled at him, he's so exasperating he's funny. Only he can make me smile when I'm severely irritated at him.

I got out of the car, turned and had to heave on the heavy car door, pushing it with my hip to get it to latch.

I bent down to the window, "You know Alex, this thing is a death trap." I threw a shrewd smirk back at him, my alter ego resurfacing.

"Ha-ha! Vi, this thing could survive anything."

"Obviously! You are behind the wheel." Standing, I patted the hood indicating he could leave any time.

His eyes shifted from my face to something behind me, and I cringed knowing the look glazing over his face.

Without checking behind me, I leaned back down to the passenger window, I gritted my words through my teeth, "Alex, don't."

"Oh look, there is Mr. Gap himself." Speaking loudly enough, so many people could hear him.

Glaring at Alex I pointed to the exit of the parking lot, giving him the hint to leave.

"Alex, leave, please! You're embarrassing me."

"Vi, seriously, he has that same polo shirt in every damn color."

"Leave! Now!" I suppressed a giggle, finding it hard to reason with his comment. It is true.

"I might see you tonight if I get bored." I winked at him with a smirk, not being able to be totally mad. As annoying as he is, he has every reason to play up his big brother role so protectively.

"If you need a ride, or if that prick does anything Vi, you call me or Max. Promise me!"

All seriousness bled into his face.

Softly I answered, "Of course Alex, and I'll be fine! Now let me get to my Gap man."

I smiled at my brother, receiving a touch of one back. I stood, and bit my lip to strangle the remainder of my grin before turning my back on the car and walked towards Billy. On my first step in Billy's direction, I heard the blue beast squeal it's tires and take off with everybody looking in our direction.

CHAPTER 4

Turning three shades of red, I reached Billy. He stood at the bottom of the entrance stairs with his hands shoved in his jean pockets, waiting for me.

"Hey Violet."

Billy is all sorts of billboard model fantasies. And yes, Alex is right, I think he has bought every color in one style of polo. Tight around the biceps and pecs and, well, all over.

Turning around to look at the dust cloud still lingering behind me, I started on the annoying apology I now had to make.

"Sorry Billy. That was my brother, trying hard to embarrass me."

Billy smiled and put his arm around me.

"Alex is your brother? Really, it's fine. I'm actually

impressed, that's an awesome car."

Oh My God, did he just say that? What is with guys and that awful car??

Billy boldly grabbed my hand and started to walk up the stairs. I knew he was forward, and with my lack of experience I didn't know if I should have been comfortable with his show of, what? Affection?

Walking around the line of people waiting to get their tickets, he slowed down in front of me, to work our way through the crowd. With one look back at me, I remembered why I agreed to this date. With just one look, he can turn his big blue eyes on you and twist them into a soft emotion that would make any girl lose the one ounce of self-respect she had left.

I looked down hiding the blush creeping into my cheeks.

"Come on Violet, I want to show you off to a few guys I know over here." He says to me with a wink.

I looked up and of course, there were two molds of Billy waving at us to come over. A red head, same build as Billy, and a blonde who seems a little taller than the other two. He was also more chiseled, wearing a tight white t-shirt that left nothing for the imagination. I tried hard not to observe his obvious self-obsession, thinking he is the form Hercules himself.

Great, standing next to a Greek God, just what I needed to boost my self-esteem.

As soon that thought came and went, two girls appeared, huddled together beside the two guys Billy was talking to. The brunette was looking at us, while the blonde boldly gawked not believing what she was seeing.

Both of them were sculpted from a stereotypical cheerleader stencil. I've seen them in school, but never spoke to them. And they never spoke to me. A situation I was quite comfortable with.

"Hey Brad! Hunter, did you catch the score of the football game?"

"Yeah I caught the score on my cell phone a minute ago...."

Drowning out that whole conversation I scanned the area around us. Many people I recognized from school were here, all of them seemed to have their eyes on us. I felt like the one thing that didn't belong in the picture they were gawking at. I guess wherever Billy goes, and who he goes with, will always bring gossip. Tomorrow it will be about me. Not something I'm looking forward to.

"Violet?"

I turned my attention back to Billy.

"I hope you don't mind, I already bought our tickets online so we didn't have to wait in line. There is always a lineup on Friday nights."

He led me by my hand, again, toward the lobby. I wasn't sure how to react towards him, but a stirring of annoyance was forming in the pit of my stomach.

While walking behind him, since he was walking faster than I could keep up, I tried to come up with something to say.

"You did? Uh...that was...nice of you. What movie?"

He gave me back my hand so that he could get his cell phone from his pocket. Letting the theatre attendant scan the tickets from the screen, Billy slid his free hand down my arm and invited himself to weave his fingers between mine. His knowing smile, that maybe worked on some girls, was making me flush red over my cheeks. Even though I battled with how a real date is supposed to go, I knew that I was just not the groveling over the hot guy type he obviously expects me to be. My irritation level was starting to climb. Sitting near a campfire, while choking on smoke, seemed like it might have been a better plan.

I went along with him, trying to think of a non-direct way to free my hand. Before I had a chance, he was pulling me towards theatre five, fingers still knitted with mine. The poster outside the door showed a picture of an adaptation of 'A modern twist of Shakespeare's Romeo and Juliet'. Just what the world needs, another Romeo and Juliet movie. My inner voice sighing and rolling her eyes.

Before we were about to go in through the theatre door, Billy slowed his pace to tease a fellow football player about who was winning the game that Hunter had reported on. I found my chance to break free from his hand, and slowly continued towards door. My eyes were on the poster as I came to a stop, waiting for Mr. Social Butterfly. He was behind me before I could decide whether I should go in without him, or turn around to get his attention. Billy put his hand around my waist while he whispered into my ear.

"I thought this would be a movie you would like. All I've ever seen you do is read, and in Mr. Thorn's English class I remember you eating up the Shakespeare stuff. Plus the story is supposed to be romantic right? Do I score brownie points?"

Sounding blissful about his choice, I was wondering if he was asking me my opinion or having a conversation with himself. Very romantic, especially where they both commit suicide. Call me a pessimist, but a love story shouldn't end in death.

"I wonder how it ends." I mumbled as I reluctantly let him lead me in to the dark room.

Billy ushered me up the stairs to a cluster of seats in the upper corner section of the theatre. He had his arm around my shoulders as soon as we sat down. The lights dimmed almost instantly, leaving me grateful for the lack of small talk between us. I was feeling smothered enough as it was.

By the time Romeo was telling Mercutio that the idea of attending the feast was a bad idea, I became attuned to my body language. I was trying to avoid Billy's arm subconsciously, not that my logic disagreed. His hand was slowly rubbing its way to the base of my neck. In doing so, I was bringing myself away from his hand, but unfortunately bringing myself closer to his torso.

My first thought was to distract him with the idea of popcorn. As I quickly turned to suggest this, drawing a breath in to speak, he took advantage of the situation without hesitation. Completely catching me off guard.

Everything happened before I could collect my thoughts. His lips were on mine, and his hand was cupping the back of my neck making it very difficult to break away without making a total scene. His other hand found its way to my cheek, pulling me into something more intrusive. I don't know if it was a panicked reaction to this type of kiss, or if the situation with him was in fact like rubbing against sandpaper, but nothing about him felt natural. It sent me to my breaking point.

Putting both my hands on his chest, I shoved him away with a little too much force. I pulled back, and saw the shock and confusion written on his face. Anger bubbled up in me, impulse driving me to get up out of my seat and pushing me down the dimly lit stairs. I pushed through the metal door without looking behind me, I was done caring. I decided my best option was to walk away from all of this. It was the type of confrontation I wanted to really avoid, otherwise confront head on. It's a knee jerk instinct for me to run, and a trained instinct for me to confront. I headed toward the lobby. Not quite reaching the crowds lingering there, I heard him behind me.

"Wait up. Violet, what's wrong? Violet! Get. Back. Here!" Frustration soaking in his last words. He was obviously searching for drama in front of everyone here.

I kept walking, my fists clenching at my sides, and my insides vibrating with anger.

"Violet! Come on, we were having fun." He yelled almost amusingly, like the joke was on me.

I stopped, my back to him with my eyes closed. I might be shy most of the time, but I do have my brother's temper. I took a breath and turned around. He was leaning against the wall, smug that I stopped in my tracks. He crossed his arms with a smirk, waiting for me to return back to him. Everyone's eyes were on me since he was purposely yelling loud enough for everyone coming in or out of the lobby to hear.

I took a couple steps in his direction, and halted my steps afraid what I'd do if I was in reaching distance of him. All my lessons rushing to my mind of how to bring down your opponent the fastest. My words came out low and seething with anger, letting them slap him instead of my hand.

"Billy, why did you ask me out? We obviously are two different types of people. You know I read. The only reason you don't know anything else about me is because you only talk about yourself. Not once have you tried to get to know me. Just in case you haven't realized, most people our age, READ."

My head was spinning, I didn't know whether to yell at him or run away to cry, but I wouldn't give anybody here the satisfaction of the latter.

My words didn't budge his unaffected grin, and laid back stance.

I decided to play his game, so I stood back on my heels and crossed my arms, mirroring his show. I raised my voice, so the audience could now hear me and really enjoy the show.

"You practically begged me to go out with you, and for what? So you could attack my face with what I can only assume was supposed to be a kiss. I'm not looking to be drooled on by a dog!" This seemed to have hit him with shock.

I found his weaknesses, his reputation and the fact that he thought I was a meek kitten. My ego flared with pride, 'I'm not so shy now, am I?' it crooned in my head.

The area was silent where we stood, except for a few

snickers coming from behind me.

Billy, brushed my comments off, finally pulling himself up off the wall, trying to regain his composure.

"Wow, you know, there are many girls who'd love to be on a date with me and in your shoes. You should be grateful I asked you in the first place."

My anger spiked, reacting on pure adrenalin. I bent down and took off my flats, which always sat at the back of my closet because they just weren't me, and I catapulted one, and then the other at him.

"Here, you can have my shoes. Go find a girl who doesn't mind your empty words and loves to hear you talk about yourself." The first shoe he didn't expect, and it hit his chest with a thud. The second, he was ready for and he deflected the strike.

"Go find someone stupid enough to fill them!"

I turned around, and realized the whole lobby was gaping at us. I ignored the cell phones pointed at me, along with the onset of applause and whoops, and violently walked out the doors. Barefoot.

I decided I better go buy something for my bare feet. In hindsight, losing my shoes might not have been the best idea. However, it was definitely affective.

I walked into the mall, and was glad to see the first shop I came across lined with racks of flip flops. I grabbed a black thinned strap pair, paid for them, then wandered down the mall. It had only been twenty minutes, just long enough for the flame of my anger to fade.

The stores were starting to close for the night, realizing it was close to nine o'clock, I started thinking about how I was going to get home. I figured I might as well join Max and Alex. My night couldn't possibly get any worse, tolerating their friends shouldn't be hard. Plus, Max would be there to talk to while Alex was off acting like a fool.

I slid my cell phone out of my back pocket, realizing I had forgotten that I had turned it off for the movie. The screen lit up, and I tried calling both my parents' cell phones since they were going to pick me up later this evening. There was no answer on either phone.

I walked back to the theater entrance. The sun had just set, the sky being on the cusp of dark, but still light enough to see around the parking lot. I wondered if it was still early enough to call Alex to come back and pick me up. My fingers decided before my mind had, and his name was up on my screen dialing out. He answered on the first ring.

"Vi, are you ok? What did HE do?"

"Alex, relax, I'm fine. I hate interrupting your thing tonight, but do you think you'd be able to pick me up at the mall?"

"Seriously Vi, if he put a hand on you, I will beat the crap out of him!" I could tell right then that he hadn't stopped thinking about me since he dropped me off.

"I handled it Alex. I told you I would."

"What. Did. He. Do." Alex's voice was low, tightness caressing his words firmly. Almost frightening me with his fierceness.

"It's fine..." I sighed. "I'd really just like to go back to being invisible. I just want to hang out with you guys tonight." My voice dissolving on the last half of my request.

"I'll be there in ten minutes..."

"Alex, don't rush..." I didn't get to tell him to take his time before there was nothing on the other end. He had already hung up.

I walked back to the theatre entrance to sit and wait for the blue beast to hurl itself around the corner. Max was seething mad, I knew he stormed away from the party, and that was the last thing I wanted.

Memories sifted through my mind of that night two years ago. I sat on a bench behind some trees, next to the stairs down to the parking lot. I dwelled on how rotten this night was and how much trouble Alex and Max will cause when they get here. I knew Max would be with him, and just as angry at Billy. My two protectors, I will always be a vulnerable little sister to them.

People came and went. I was really hoping not to see Billy, I couldn't face seeing him again tonight. I don't have any spirit left, my anger has left me limp and cold. I just wanted to get out of here.

Thirty minutes had passed and I was starting to wonder why Alex hadn't come yet. The old military base was just up the highway from here. I pulled out my cell phone to give him another call, and to tease him that I might as well start walking there. This time, his phone went right to voicemail. I tried my parents again, and still couldn't get through. So I flipped through the phone call log to find Max's number. He'd be with Alex, at least I'd get to tease one of them.

There was a brief and awkward silence before I heard, "Hi."

A rough voice answered shades too dark to be Max.

"Hey, uhh… is this Max?" The question came out of me more as a confused mumble.

"Yeah. Vi. It's me. Where are you?" It wasn't really a question, more of an urgent statement.

"Waiting outside of the theatre for Alex to pick me up, but he is fashionably late, as usual."

"Stay there, I'm coming to pick you up."

"What? Why? Don't worry about me Max, Alex will show up eventually. You don't have to leave the party for me."

"No. Vi, I'm not at the party. I'm on my way. You need to come with me. Alex got in an accident on the highway."

Panic rose in my voice. "WHAT? Max, what is going on? Where is Alex?"

"I'm pulling in to the parking lot right now, I'll be right there."

Then the phone went silent, and his S.U.V. neared in a loud accelerated roar.

KISS OF AFFLICTION

CHAPTER 5

One of the neon ceiling lights flickered while a fly flew around trying to catch it. I'm not sure which was worse, sitting on the most uncomfortable chairs for four hours, or the silence of the unknown. My leg violently bobbed up and down venting some of my anxiety.

Max, put his hand on my knee to calm me down.

He hadn't said much on the way here. Just that Kendra, had come up to him at the party telling him that Alex left in a rage. Max got in his Jeep and followed the settling dust trail to the highway, and turned toward the movie theaters figuring something was up with me. He came up to a cop car along the highway, an accident in the background. The officer on the scene knew Max and told him it was Alex. That's when I called, and the officer told him to go pick me up and get me immediately to the hospital. Neither one of us knew the condition of my brother.

In the midst of our strained silence, Max said he figured Alex's car was a write off. My heart attacked my throat at the thought of the beast being injured beyond repair. Alex's voice playing in my head "This thing can survive anything."

In the middle of the vacant waiting room, I turned to Max and tried so hard to keep my head in what was happening.

"Max, I am going to freak, I need to know what's going on. Where is Alex? Why won't they let me in to see him? Even if he is bad, I still want to see him."

Tears of frustration and fear started down my face. I can't remember the last time I allowed myself to cry.

Max tiredly put his arms around me to try and sooth me. All I knew is that if someone didn't take me to my brother I was going to go out of my mind.

"I've tried calling your parents, but there isn't any answer, do you know where they are tonight?"

Pulling away I had realized Mom and Dad didn't know.

"Oh My God, I completely forgot to call them! Before I called Alex, I was trying their cell phones, but there was no answer. They must have forgotten them at home. They should be home now wondering why I wasn't at the mall to get picked up."

Max handed me a tissue box that was sitting on a table beside him.

"I think they had a charity dinner at the Boat Club down on the wharf." Thinking about it, they never really said much about where they were going, or maybe I hadn't paid attention if they had.

"Ok, you stay here, I'll go outside and try to call them. Reception in here is bad."

I nodded my head as he wrapped his hoodie around my shoulders.

Panic started to set in as I watched Max's back go out the door automatic doors.

I started to raise out of my chair to head towards the nurse's station, wanting to ask for information for the hundredth time. Before I could take my first step, a handful of police officers walked through the same automatic doors to the emergency room. They went straight to the receptionist. It didn't register as odd to see police in a hospital, but it was slightly odd that there were seven of them. They all looked as exhausted as I felt.

Then they all started looking at me while the receptionist was pointing my way. Panic was spreading down into my fingers as I felt my heart lobbing out of my chest. I stumbled back down into my seat.

Max, coming in, caught what I was focused on. He eyed the group of police as he walked past them, and continued over to me. His head shook as he approached in what I thought maybe was disbelief, then he leaned against the wall to my right. I felt his gaze between me and the cops.

The same officer who spoke to the secretary, started my way, while the others kept their distance.

"Violet?" I've met the man many times before, just not in uniform. The police officer is Kendra's father.

"Mister Vautour." My mouth was dry. His name was all I could get passed my lips.

"Violet, what do you know about what happened tonight?" His voice was very tender as he sat where Max had been sitting earlier.

I tried to bring my voice up past my throat.

"Alex was on his way to pick me up at the mall and was in a car accident." I nervously looked down at my hands fidgeting with a thread from the hem of my cut off shorts. "I am waiting for someone to tell me how he is doing."

I looked back up at Kendra's Dad. There was a tortured expression in his eyes, but he kept all emotion off his face. I expected it being a requirement of his job.

Breaking our silent, hollow stare, he looked over at the other cops standing by the door. One of them came over, glancing at me as though he didn't know where to place his eyes, and handed Mr. Vautour a manila envelope.

"You were informed correctly. Your brother hit a car head on. We don't know why he swerved into the oncoming lane. We still have officers on the scene, and we will have specialists out in the morning to do a reconstruction to determine the cause. This is typical in these situations."

"Oh." I blanked. The truth in his words was like a punch to my stomach, I forced air back into my lungs.

"Do you know how my brother is? Have the doctors told you anything about his condition? They won't tell me anything. I really want to go in and see him." My panic was starting to heighten.

"Violet, your brother…" He shifted his legs toward me uncomfortably.

"The accident was one of the worse I have ever came upon. He was unconscious when we arrived and had multiple issues when the ambulance took him. The doctors are trying to stop the bleeding from the internal damage. Violet, it's not looking good for him."

Every part of my body froze. Even if I wanted to react, I couldn't. I kept starring at the police officer next to me, not knowing how to absorb his words. He looked unsure, waiting for the smallest understanding from me. I had nothing to give him.

"Violet, listen to me, I know you are feeling a lot emotionally right now, it's a lot to take in."

Kendra's Dad was struggling to find his voice. He gently put his hand on my wrist which was keeping a rock solid fist on my lap.

"The vehicle that he hit…" He closed his eyes and slowly started speaking, forcing every word out.

"He was going well over the speed limit, the vehicle that Alex hit was fatal. They died instantly. Violet…" Mr Vautour cleared the knot in his throat.

"It was your parent's vehicle."

In that moment everything was stripped from me.

I sat, staring at him blindly with the room spinning

around me. Not understanding, not knowing what the words he spoke meant. Everything around me felt so far away and muted.

The usual movements my body would make automatically, I now had to put thought into. This moment couldn't afford thought. To think, to understand, to digest any idea was dangerous. I couldn't allow that gate to open, so I kept it firmly shut with my sight on my hands in my lap.

I thought I heard Max yelling, but I couldn't make out what he was saying or who he was saying it to. Everything was a distant scene happening in slow motion around me. The nurse at the nurse's station, the backup of cops, the doctor walking in to see what was going on, or Mr. Vautour. With my head in my hands, I folded over my thighs.

Two of the cops standing near the sliding ER door approached Max. He had repositioned himself within inches in front of me as if he were shielding me from the dread that was waiting on the other side. This gradually pulled me out of my comatose state. Two of the officers held his arms behind his back telling him to calm down or they'd have to sedate him. Those words just spread the fire in him even further, and I caught the words. "Don't touch her!" spitting from his lips.

Officer Vautour walked around Max, his eyes set on me as I slowly started to look through my blurred vision to everything happening in front of me. He held his hand out so I would take it to go with him. Automatically, my mind lunged at the idea of being torn away from Max.

Abruptly, Max exhausted himself and quietly dropped to his knees, burying his head in my lap with breaking sobs vibrating down his back. I looked up at the officers still holding him from behind. Making eye contact with me, they freed his arms which limply found their way around me. I felt him take a shaky deep breath, then he hastily pulled himself from my legs and gathered my torso to his large frame, pulling me tightly in to his chest.

Slowly, the hell of what was happening started to seep in. My heart increasingly became shattered and heavy as led. With Max holding on to me so tight, I realized the story I was given was now my horrible truth.

"No. Max...no.... they can't be gone...." I was trying to push him away while words barely forming, air coming out of my mouth as uncontrollable sobs instead of words.

"Vi, I'm right here."

"Max, No." I limply pushed him back to see it in his eyes.

The world shook. It didn't spin in circles, it wasn't spinning. It shook me from the inside out with aggression and pain. I got up and tried to run from it, trying to find a spot that didn't pulse erratically everywhere. My mind shut down and I let my emotions drive my body. Screaming and sobbing frantically trying to catch my breath, but I was far from my instinctive natural abilities. I found myself in the back corner of the waiting room, crouched against the cool walls, wrapped around my knees attempting to make it all still. I pulled my tear soaked eyes up from my knees seeing Max's back side. He stood blocking anyone who tried to come near me, his delirium returning with mine.

His tortured eyes caught mine at the end of one of my tortured wails. Our emotions bleeding together. A hand pulled on his arm, the sea of professionals at the ready to help in how they felt best. Max spun around connecting his clenched fist to the officer's jaw with full force, throwing Mr. Vautour back, but not to the ground. The other men started toward us in a fast rush, Max's stance was ready to fight them all. Kendra's Dad held them all back.

Max turned, then was down on the floor with me, picking me up and walking over to a bench against the wall. He held me on his lap and I let the darkness take over me completely.

As I sunk deeper, anchored to the depth of my affliction, his voice rumbled through his chest, "She stays with me."

Then the world, and everything in it, was gone.

I started to wake from the dizzying fog inside my head and the smell told me that I was in the hospital. The pungent scent of disinfectant mixed with the stink of hospital food and stale coffee made my weak stomach want to heave. I slowly pulled my heavy eyelids open.

I was laying on a stiff vinyl sofa in one of the waiting rooms on the 5th floor. I assume it was since there was a big black number '5' painted on the light green brick walls.

It was quiet here, nobody around but Max. My head rested on his thigh, with his hoodie shoved under my head. I felt the heat from his hand resting on my ribs. I couldn't move. Any ounce of energy I had, had been spent.

My throat was swollen and dry, only a gravely whisper would come out.

"Max?"

"Vi? Do you need anything?" Max's hand started to stroke my hair trying to warm the chill that filled me.

My tears started to fall onto his jeans, marking wet dots until a bunch became one.

"Is it all true?"

"I wish I could tell you it is all a really bad dream. What the officer said about the accident, it's true." He looked down at me with blood shot eyes.

I wondered how long I was unconscious. How long he sat here holding me crying in his own torment.

My parents are gone. They are dead.

I closed my eyes and tried to hold back the creeping hysteria that threatened to return.

"What about Alex?" My voice cracked trying to get out my brother's name.

It really seemed like someone is playing Russian roulette with my family, and I am losing in a big way.

"He is still critical. He came out of his last surgery about twenty minutes ago and the doctor said it could go either way. They have done as much as they can for now."

I closed my eyes wishing I could be void of the blazing emotions churning inside me. Leaving me feeling like I need to pull myself apart to alleviate this deep pain. I wasn't equipped for this. My brother accidentally killed my parents. It was hard to even think that thought without sharp fear ripping my mind apart.

I want to feel anger, but I can't direct it at my brother, especially not when all I can do is panic over the thought of losing him too. The moment I start to feel even a slight flicker of anger, the spark smolders reminding me I was the one who called him in the first place. He was coming to pick me up. One moment sooner, one moment later and this entire situation would have been completely different. If I had not called him at all, if I would have just got a taxi and went home.

A doctor cleared his throat, entering the private waiting room. I was coiled into Max's arms, holding on to him so I wouldn't let myself shatter. I couldn't see the doctor, but I could hear him sit on the seat across from us. I had to hear what he had to say, no matter how much my soul threatened to splinter. I brought myself up off of Max, slumping in the seat beside him. The doctor's eyes fixated on me in concentration.

"How are you feeling Violet?"

I shook my head, not daring to speak a word or my feeble attempt at control will come crashing down.

Max spoke up, sensing my restraint and the off chance I could break once more. The idea of me being knocked out with a sedative again prompted him to speak up.

"How is he?"

"Alex is out of surgery, and is in recovery. He is being monitored closely by our staff, as we previously discussed. We were able to stop most of the bleeding, but his alcohol level was high, which made it very difficult to control the repair. We've done all that we can do for him for now."

A silent panic hit me with full force, the room starting to do what the other waiting room had done before.

"I thought Violet would like to hear it from me. Do you have any questions for me? I want to be at your disposal." He said setting his clipboard on his lap.

Again, I shook my head. I probably should have something to ask him, but nothing was being absorbed or processed.

"Would you like to go see your brother?" The doctor was looking at me, then shifted his questioning eyes to Max.

I could hardly sit in my body, I wanted to scream and yell, throw a tantrum and completely get out of my head. Instead, I shoved it all in. I nodded my head with a tear silently falling down my face.

Walking the hall to his intensive care unit was like walking on water. My body was responding to what it needed to do, without any communication from my hollowed heart or numbed mind. I had no idea how it was happening, just that it was.

The white jacket in front of us, stopped at room 5993. I grabbed Max's hand and held on terrified at what we might see. The doctor started opposing that Max enter the room, only immediate family was allowed visitation. With a torn, frustrated, look on my face, my eyes bored into his.

"Immediate family? Alex and Max are what is left of my immediate family. Max is the only thing keeping me together, and I need him in there with me. He is our brother, blood or not."

The doctor's face registered the hint of threat laced in my tone, and took a step back and let us both in.

We walked in to the dimmed recovery room. Alex was laying in the hospital bed, his head heavily bandaged. Many machines hooked up to him were showing rhythmic lines and making measured noises. A ventilator tube protruded out of his mouth, the machine pumping air into his lungs. Machines are keeping him here with us.

Everything I had known. Everything in my life. He is all that I am able to hold on to out of all of this. There's nothing left without him.

Love is too short of a word, too simple, maybe even abrasive. Love can never be strong enough to compare to the loss I feel in my soul. Love.

Life is so much more than a birthday card written with love before your name. Alex is my brother, my friend, and now I know he is much more to me than those simple things. He was in everything I did, everything I am, and I had planned on him being in everything I was supposed to be.

How foolish of me to think it would have gone that easily, taking it all for granted like it was assumed everything would always be the same.

I sat down in the wood chair beside the bed.

He lay in front of me, motionless, lifeless except for the continuous mechanical breathing given to him by the machine. I took his hand and held it to my face. It was cold against my warm tears. I could smell his scent on his skin. So many memories stir with the hint of that one scent. It kept him alive in this moment for me.

Looking up through my tear stained eyes, Max huddled to himself leaning against the wall, his hands to his eyes.

"Max?" I broke into his thoughts with my quivering voice.

Wiping his eyes he looked up at me with a face that had lost all hope.

"Yeah?"

"I don't know what to do, what am I supposed to say?"

He pulled the hem of his t-shirt up to dry his face. Then grabbed another chair from across the room, and sat next to me. His hand covered mine and Alex's resting on the edge of the bed.

"I guess we just talk to him. Tell stories, be with him. Threaten him that we won't leave until he wakes up."

Max looked over at Alex, with the touch of a smirk in hopes that he'd overhear the threat.

Very quietly, two nurses came in to do what they said was routine work. They asked if we would wait out in the hallway until they were done. Neither of us were willing to leave, but they pushed us along to head to the kitchen which they said has a coffee machine and fridge. Not that I was hungry, but I caved on the suggestion of a coffee.

"We will only be about ten minutes, and then you are welcome to come back in with him. I can come down and get you when we are finished." The middle aged nurse sported a very short haircut which did nothing for her chubby features, but her kind face made me take to her instantly.

I left my hand on the closed door, fighting with myself to walk the twenty steps down the hall.

The coffee tasted horrible, but felt good on my swollen, sore throat. I leaned against the wall waiting for the machine to brew Max's coffee. I looked out the window over the one table set in here. It was still very early in the morning, and I couldn't see much through the blackness of the night. The smell of coffee filled the cramped space as the liquid streamed into the Styrofoam cup.

"Did you want cream Vi?" Max asked, walking over to the fridge.

Digging around inside, he mumbled, "If there is any."

Barely audible, I heard the high pitch noise of a constant beep. Then sounds of running steps turning the corner, and running past the closed door of the kitchenette. My coffee sliding out of my hand, spilling all over the glossy floor.

I followed the team of doctors and nurses down the hall. I screamed Alex's name running down the hall, then saw them go into his room. I didn't have to ask what was wrong with him, there was nothing more than the worst case scenario that could happen. I was headed into the room, but Max grabbed me and launched me to a stop with me screaming and crying in his chest.

"We can't help him Vi."

He kept repeating to me until it sunk in, and I leaned back on the room window that faced the hallway. My forehead pressed against the glass.

Time passed slowly, but far too quickly. I tried everything to block out the noise of the constant beep searing itself into my brain. We stood holding each other, his arms around me, his head resting on the side of mine watching the horror show in front of us.

I felt a cold hand on my shoulder. I turned my head to see the doctor standing beside us. Before he could say anything, the two same nurses we just left in the room were bringing their cart out. Behind them I could see no movement coming from the machines that Alex was attached to.

Max caught me before my body gave in to the weight of the enormity of my situation. My entire body wanted to collapse in on itself. The echoes of my grief were horrifying for me to even process that I was wailing. With every heart splintering emotion lapping over me, I'd let out another cry. Max held me from behind and didn't let go until I sobbed myself into exhaustion.

The only words he'd say through his own tears were, "I won't let go, Vi."

Max hooked his arm under my legs and picked me up.

"I need to get you out of here before they come at you with another needle to knock you out."

Walking down the hallway with me in his arms I begged him not to take me away from Alex and my parents. I cried on him furiously again, shattering everything inside me. My thoughts escaped my howling sobs.

"I should be dead too." I said into his shirt.

"I'm so sorry Vi, we can't stay here. Hey will just medicate you, and there is no way I'm going to let that happen."

I was emotionally paralyzed. The infecting mass of emotions were too much to bare. They blocked everything out and locked everything in. My body was my tomb, everyone I loved was gone and I had nothing but too much inside me.

The next time I looked up we were alone in an elevator.

"Do you want to go to my place or yours?" He asked through his own silent tears.

The realization that I had nothing to go home to, nobody waiting for me there, cruelly washed over me. I buried into Max's chest letting out a short series of sobs, and spoke into it. "Yours."

CHAPTER 6

The gazebo's spring hinged screen door creaked open, breaking my horrible recollection of what felt like someone else's life. I looked up to see Max standing in the doorway holding coffees and a white paper bag. He stood staring at me, his dark hair dripping from the downpour outside.

I wondered what he saw through those brown eyes that made him look so concerned. The rawness of my throat made me realize I was trying hard not to cry, and being very unsuccessful in my pursuit.

"I knew I shouldn't have left you after the nightmares you had last night."

"I'm fine Max." I was surprised at how hollow my words came out, more so than usual lately, which I didn't think possible.

I sat up to give him a spot to sit beside me.

"The coffee smells good, thanks for grabbing some."

Patting the cushion beside me, he finally broke out of whatever he was contemplating, and sat down on the couch.

I tried to explain the basics of what I could put into words, to help him understand what he just saw written on my face when he walked in.

"Max, I feel completely spent. When I try to remember I am either stabbed with intense pain where I physically want to double over, or I become vividly lost inside my own head. Everything in you, you've given it all to me. I want you to know that I have seen all that you've done for me, it's not lost on me."

He let out a breath releasing the tension he had been holding on to, and put his feet up on the coffee table.

"Max, I don't think I'm being a very good friend. I should be doing the same for you. I feel like you're all I've got right now. If I screw something up, promise me you will tell me. You are like a brother to me, and I can't lose you too."

Last week those words didn't hold the same meaning as they do now. They are much more profound and everlasting in my mind. Max is whatever that position holds, as new and misunderstanding as it is, it is as deep as my soul and I'm offering it to him.

He passed me my coffee from the coffee shop at the end of the street. Taking a sip of his steaming coffee, he looked at me. His arm rested along the backside of the couch.

"This is all I want, Vi. I think this is what we both

want. Time. I need time alone, but when I am alone, I don't know... I can't just sit there. I thought staying away from you those first couple of days would help you. Help not remember so much, I didn't want to be the cause of any more pain. I could hear you during the night, waking yourself up from your nightmares and I felt paralyzed. I didn't know what to do for you."

He paused to take another drink, and stared at the lid.

"I don't want to be lonely, and maybe that's selfish of me. I can't stand not knowing how you are or what you are doing when I'm not close. You get what I'm feeling right now. Just being with you is what I need. I don't know how to explain it beyond that."

Time slid by while we cocooned ourselves in, mutually hurting and hollow. Max would get up to poke at the fire and put a new log on, we stayed comfortable in our sorrow.

I don't think there are too many people in this world who have felt what I have felt these past few days. It is a little different for Max. They weren't his parents, although he was close to them. Alex was his best friend. His future can still keep on down the same path.

"I hate this! I never know what I want, if I want to sleep or not, if I am hungry or not, if I want to be here or not. Everything is so messed up." I blurted out in a random angry verbal spasm.

"Yeah. I know what you mean."

Not that it was bright out, it was a very dull day, but it seemed like it was starting to dim around us. I don't know where the day had disappeared to. Another day down and

I managed through it. Sobering me up from my anger a little.

"Shoot, I forgot about the bagels, sorry." Max reached for the white paper bag sitting on the table, and offered me one. A cold toasted bagel wasn't going to do much to help my appetite return. I thought back, but couldn't remember the last time I ate something.

"It's alright, thanks though. I'm not really hungry."

We went back to our easy silence, spellbound by the fire. The rain came down hard around our shelter.

"Max, what were you and Alex doing, the last time you were with him."

Before I could reel my words back into my mouth he began to answer it. I didn't mean to bring up any memories, good or bad. I didn't know if I could handle hearing what he had to say.

"Uhmm…" He cleared his throat, taking his time to collect his thoughts.

"We were out at the base. We had set up the tents, actually I set them up. Alex was getting lots of attention from Jenn and Emma, so I let him off the hook, and set them up on my own."

I turned my head to look at Max's half grinning face.

"Jenn and Emma from math class?" The girls were nice enough, they'd say hi to me when passing by them in the hallways at school. Emma had straight bleach blonde hair, always wearing a bright color of skinny jeans. Jennifer wore glasses, with her curly shoulder length rust color hair bouncing around in tight spirals. I remember in grade eight, one of her lenses came out of her frames and she had to sit in the office waiting for her mother to arrive. She couldn't see to walk around the school, let alone stay in class.

The duo were always enthusiastically happy, which made them perfect for the spirit committee. Kendra was president for senior year, and knew Jenn and Emma well.

He let out a deep chuckle.

"Yeah, those two. By the time I was finished putting up both tents, it was almost dark and Alex had started a fire in our pit. You've never been out there before, have you? It's kind of set up in sections, each area has its own wheel rim for a fire. I went to the cooler to get a beer, and it was half empty. Every time Alex went to get a beer, he'd get one for the girls too."

Max's quiet chuckle echoed through the sofa. Clearing his conflicted mind, he rubbed his hands over his unshaven face and set them, fingers locked, behind his head looking into the fire.

"There were a lot of people around, lots of people you usually hang out with. Kendra was even there, looking disgusted that her friends were so focused on Alex. She came over and asked me if I had convinced you to come to the party after your date. I totally would have tried talking you out of it, if I had of known."

The lightness from the memories relaxed the creases on his face that I thought would permanently be engraved there. His eyes were set on me in his naturally intrigued way. Not the sad or dutiful way, like they have been recently. The old Max was peeking through, for now. The arch of his eyebrow implied he was waiting for me to say something.

I squirmed a bit, knowing he'd want the full story.

"Ok, fine. I was on a date with Billy West. He had been asking me out for a while, so I finally caved and said yes. It wasn't anything serious, we just went to a movie. Well, we were supposed to anyway."

Max stared at me contemplating something. I thought for sure he'd start making fun of me like Alex had. At this point, nothing could affect either one of us. If a meteor fell in this backyard, it would hold no shock value. We were too emotionally exhausted.

I turned to sit sideways on the couch and broke his silence, I knew it was coming anyway.

"I know, I know... YES, Billy, that Billy. The whole thing confirmed what you both thought of him. He apparently thought I was just like all the other girls he's taken out, and was only there to make out with him. I walked out of the movie mid-way through and he followed me to the lobby."

"What happened?" Max spoke straight faced looking into the fire.

"He started showing off in front of everyone, yelling at me to be grateful. I lost it. I totally flipped out at him. I made a scene in front of everyone, I couldn't stop myself. He was being such a self-centered moron. He told me that there were many girls that would love to be in my shoes, so I threw mine at him and told him to go find someone else to fill them. I had to go into the mall and buy new ones. " I couldn't help chuckling at the thought.

"You really threw your shoes at Billy West?" Leaning forward he shoved his empty coffee cup in the cardboard tray it came in, and tried to subdue the smile spreading on his face.

"I mean, I get why all the girls at school grovel over him, he's all hunky, but I don't get why he'd think I'd be like them. I'm sure there are a few videos online of the episode. You can youtube it."

"I can't believe he had the balls to try you like that."

"Well, I wondered why he kept asking me to go out with him. He's built to be a model, and well, I'm just me. We have nothing in common. I knew it wouldn't work, but one date would have been nice. It's not like I have guys lining up at my door."

"Vi, you weren't seriously attracted to that meat head were you?"

Without answering his question, I looked at him and he indulged me with some answers.

"About a month ago, we were at the school's football game against St. Andrews High School. Long story short Alex was flirting with the cheerleaders from the other team and invited a few of them out afterwards. One of them was Billy's ex and, well, put two and two together. Billy might have been asking you out to get back at Alex. You know how protective he was over you. I'm not saying that's why Billy was into you, but I'm sure getting Alex all worked up over you going out with him would be a bonus."

"I don't think Billy was ever into me. I should have

known better."

"No, it's not like that." He shifted his body beside me so we were facing each other, obviously getting ready to give me some in depth explanation.

"Vi, you don't get the effect you have under that nerdy, quiet routine of yours. You're all cool comfortable in who you are and how you do things. It's not about how hard some girls try to be beautiful, the ones who catch a guy's attention are the ones who are naturally beautiful. Not just that, you are into interesting things. What other girl would want to sit all day and watch all of the Avengers movies? Or go to a concert, not to party, but because you love the music? Nobody should have to try to be someone they aren't, and it's never even crossed your mind to be anybody but who you are. Why do you think Alex was so protective over you? You are the coolest chick I know."

I nudged his arm with my shoulder and a laugh, "I'm cool? I think lack of sleep is catching up with your ability to think clearly."

He smiled back.

"So many times Alex has threatened guys to stay away from you. He'd never let them get close to you because he knew you were better than them. He wanted you to go places and see things, far from Black River and the small town minds that are here. So, Alex would make sure everyone got the hint, his little sister was not to be touched."

"Yeah... thank you Alex for leaving me with no social life." I said dryly, trying not to think about how I don't have a big circle of friends.

"The only date I've had my senior year was awful, and I was just a pawn to anger my brother. Do you know how annoying that is?" Frustrated, I pulled a sofa pillow to my front to hug.

"I know all too well Vi." He said softly, mostly to himself.

"Billy didn't think Alex would go through with the threats. Trust me, when Alex got to the campsite, his plans for revenge were already forming. He just didn't want you to be caught in the middle. So yeah, Billy used you to make Alex mad, but it's not like he, and every other guy, haven't been eyeing you like candy. Knowing you were untouchable just made it worse. How do you not see any of this Vi?"

I wasn't sure how to respond to that. I chose not to digest the compliment I'm sure he was giving me. My thoughts went to Alex and how I was always under his wing, even when I didn't know it. The conflict between irritation and loss slapped me hard, playing heavy on my weary heart. My thoughts seized my body and it was written on my face.

Somehow reading my thoughts, my hands were caught in Max's.

With his eyebrows furrowed and his gaze on his thumb stumbling around my twisted leather bracelet, he continued his story.

"I was really angry that night. Angry at Alex for leaving without me, leaving after he had drank too much. Angry at myself for letting it all happen. Alex tore out of the base in his car, and I had no idea why. I didn't even know that you were out with Billy until Alex arrived to the campsite. Kendra had come to me while I was getting ready to sit down and said that he got a call and was asking over and over 'Did he hurt you?' I knew he was pissed, and even though I had no idea what was happening, I was going to be right there with him. All I could think about was what Billy might have done to you."

I looked out the window beside us as he continued.

"I should have figured out what was going on before we headed down there that night so I could have convinced you that Billy was no good for you. The idea of him even touching you drives me insane."

Putting the pillow on Max's lap, I picked up a blanket and pulled it up around me and stayed in his warmth.

"I shouldn't have called him that night Max, I should have just waited for Dad to pick me up, or taken a taxi, or walked."

My heavy heart was regressing back to my torturous, consuming melancholy. Betraying me, tears escaped my closed eyes. I wiped them quickly and held back any more trying to take over. Not tonight. The only thing I do know is that I don't want to be completely consumed by my life.

I leaned into his arm, shivering because of my angst under my blanket.

"And I should have stopped him from getting in the car."

"Max, you know there is nothing that could have stopped Alex from picking me up. That was just Alex." My words coming out in almost a whisper.

We sank back into our rhythm of quietness, watching the fire in the fireplace slowly go out.

Max pulled his arm from the back of the couch and put it on my arm.

"Ok, so how do you feel about going inside to shower? I mean this with all the love in the world Vi, you look like crap. You've been in that dress for way too long and I know you aren't comfortable. Let's go inside, get you showered, and put something comfortable on. Then I'm going to take you out for some real food. Let's attempt a piece of normal in our life, whether we want to or not. Plus, these bagels didn't do us much good."

I slowly pulled myself up, off his lap, and sat up.

"The thought of going in the house terrifies me, but I do want to get out of this dress."

He got up and held out his hands, helping me up from the sofa and pulled me towards the door of the gazebo. Slipping his flip flops on he held open the screen door.

"And dinner? Will you come with me?"

"I probably should be hungry, but I'm not. If I make it through being able to be in the house, showering, and changing, then I will go with you. That, and because there is no way I'm staying here alone."

Unhooking his hand from mine, he rested it on the small of my back to urge me past him and the door.

"Like   I'd   ever   leave   you,   Vi."

CHAPTER 7

The clouds surrendered to the sun, and the rain had stopped with streaks of the lowering sunlight painting the back yard. The cold wet grass on my bare feet brought a few senses back to my body. I tried focusing on it rather than the terror creeping up my spine as we came to the back door of the house.

Inside, my unreachable past life still lingered. I did my best to ignore the small details of my so called life, and walked up the staircase with Max on my heels. I kept my head down, trying not to look into the eyes of all the pictures staring at me. Those happy moments, now painful reminders.

My bedroom, thankfully, still stood as it did before all this. Embracing me as it always had. The bed still in a mess from the last time I slept in it. Dirty clothes in the hamper, untouched.

Max stood in the doorway while I slowly made my way in.

"Want me to stay up here until you're done?"

I shook my head, "No, I don't think. If I start to lose it I will call you up, ok?"

He nodded with uncertainty, and headed back down the hall, to the stairs.

An adjoining bathroom connects between my brother's room and mine. Always extremely inconvenient when we both wanted to use it at the same time. Turning on the bathroom lights, the bright LEDs stunned my dried vision for a split second. I blinked a couple times, and realized I was staring straight through to Alex's room.

I froze.

All of his living things were there. Things he touched the last time he was home. They are still here, the meaningless, material things that meant something at one time. Now the only thing that matters is that he's gone.

I closed my eyes, dizzy with grief. How is it possible to physically hurt this bad? Every aching thought of him infects me like a disease. The worst part is knowing it will always hurt, no amount of time could possibly heal this suffering. Cliché to think time heals all wounds and memories fade. You replace past memories with new ones. My family could never be replaced.

Swallowing the lump in my throat, I opened my eyes and pushed myself to be numb. I walked to the other side of the room and closed his door. Locking it, along with my heart.

I kept my eyes away from the mirror, avoiding the skeleton that would have no choice but to look back at me. Working through the shower routine mechanically, forcing myself not to think about anything. I hurried through it, stepped out and wrapped my towel around my body. I wanted to be away from his door as fast as I could. Being in my bedroom was more calming than I expected it to be. Pieces of normal things comforted me, if even for brief moments.

Dripping on my carpeted floor, I walked over to the closet and swung the door open. Like usual, a mess. I put on my ripped jeans that Mom hated, but were my favorite and a staple of mine, and a black tank top. My oversized black knit cardigan was laying folded in a pile of clean clothes Mom would have sat on my dresser. My hand reached out for it and lightly ran across the top of it hoping to feel her last touch. There was nothing, she was gone.

I grabbed the sweater and left, almost running downstairs. The last twenty minutes gave me enough energy to face what Max wanted to do. Go out in public. The only good thing about his plan was that I got to leave the house.

Passing, once again, the parade of pictures hanging on the wall going down the stair case. Turning my head in the opposite direction from the smiling pictures, I caught sight of Max sitting on the couch in the living room and I hurried to join him.

"I need out of this house Max, take me anywhere, I really don't care. I can't sleep here tonight. There are too many things, too many memories. My head is filled with everything at once and it's too hard to push them out. I can't be here, I'm too exhausted."

"OK, food first. How about the little restaurant down on the wharf. We can get some fish and chips or a burger? We will worry about the where we sleep afterwards."

"Anywhere but here." I got up off the couch and headed for the entry way. Starting for the closet, I pulled back the door to find a bin full of sneakers. There was one pair I was looking for. The mangled red and white converse sneakers Alex gave me last Christmas. I've worn them practically every day since I got them. They are my favorite, and now I can't find them.

With sneakers all around me on the floor, I sat back leaning on the door case and put my head in my hands. It took all I had not to cry, but all the failed attempts of trying not to cry added to my rising temper.

"My stupid sneakers just can't be where I left them. Did someone come in here and clean?"

Taking a deep breath and sucking it up, I started digging again. I am so mad, mad at my thoughts, mad they won't go away, mad at the way I feel, mad at the situation I've been dealt.

I surrendered to the mess in the closet and turned with flip flops in hand. Max stood with my converse in hand and a playful look in his eyes, otherwise his face was serious. I took them with a mumbled thanks. Sliding my feet into them, we walked out the door.

We pulled off of the highway to a dirt road with a sign that indicated we were on course to the wharf. Max's S.U.V. hit every pot hole. At one point we caught each other's eye and he took his hand off the stick shift and put it on my thigh.

"You alright?" Turning his eyes back to the road.

"Fine…" My irritation still obvious, it seemed hard to shake. He patted my leg and returned his hand to where it naturally fit on the steering wheel.

The drive down to the wharf would have been cheerful if I had any joy in me. We were surrounded by thick forest on both sides. It felt like we were in a tunnel it was getting dark and the shade of the trees were blocking what sunlight was left in the sky. Getting closer to the wharf, the road spurted narrow lanes with little cottages built off of them.

Suddenly, the thick woods opened up to a wooden platform, bringing us to the beach. At the end of the wharf was a crafty lighthouse. It was big enough to make new comers to the beach wonder if it was real, people like me. It wasn't though, I remember hearing stories about it here. The lighthouse was part of the connecting restaurant.

"Max, I don't think I've ever been out here before. I'm sure I would remember this place."

Putting the truck into park, he pointed out the front window. Looking ahead all I could see was the very end of the wharf where water stretched out ahead. Boats were heading in to dock at the wharf before nightfall. The sun was peeking through a few rain clouds that were headed this way. It was a beautiful vision, taking my thoughts away. The view brought me to a place of solitude, and I couldn't stop staring into it. Max eventually put his hand on my shoulder and pulled me back to him. The things he has seen on my face the last few days, why he stays around me I'm not sure. I nodded to his concerned face to let him know I was fine, and turned to open the door and got out.

"Hey Max, do you mind if we just walk the wharf for a few minutes, until the sun is down."

"Sure. You should grab your sweater though, as soon as the sun goes down it will get cold pretty fast."

Getting my sweater out of his truck, a faint memory came to me. I walked back around to where he was leaning, his back against the back side of the S.U.V.

"Max, do you remember last summer when you and Alex were talking about a party on some wharf? Was it down here?"

His gaze went down to the wood planks, with a smile, Max mumbled, "Yeah."

"So what was so funny about that night, neither one of you would tell me what went on."

With a chuckle he looked out over at the row of boats and pointed in their direction.

"My Uncle's sail boat is third from the end. He owns the restaurant and docks it over there. We came here after a party at Kelly Stone's house. Apparently she didn't approve of Alex puking all over her parent's furniture. I didn't want to bring him home, especially where I was in a bad state too, so we took a cab down here. Uncle Ted put us up in his boat for the night to sleep it off. When we got in the boat, the mini fridge was packed full of beer, and the boat beside us was pretty lively."

He looked up at the sound of one of the fog horns blowing from one of the boats that had docked.

"And that's as much of what you need to know of that night. We spent the night and came home the next morning."

Shaking my head, I turned and started to walk toward the end of the dock. I sat on the last plank letting my feet dangle over the edge. The sun staring at me while starting to touch the horizon. Max followed, sitting beside me doing the same.

"Max, am I missing out on that much of my teenage life by staying home a lot? You and Alex seemed to have so much fun while I was home either not wanting to go out, or not going out because I have protectors even when I don't need protecting who scare people off." I tried to sound bothered by that fact.

"I don't think. Were you unhappy? You need to do whatever you want to make you happy. Stay home, party, makes no difference in the long run. It's the people who are with you in the end."

He took my hand and held it as we watched the sun go down. The hazy pink breath from the sun swallowed into the darkness.

Once it went down I started to get up, wrapping myself in my cardigan.

"So, at the end of the day, you enjoyed being with those two middle aged women you guys woke up next to in your Uncle's boat?" I looked at him sitting on the edge looking up at me. I cocked an inquisitive eyebrow. I turned with a satisfied smirk on my face, and started walking away.

"Word travels pretty fast in a high school Max." I spoke loudly into the wind, allowing it to travel back to him. His stunned stare on my back caused me to slow down and look his way. Finally he hopped up and caught up to me, putting his arm around my shoulders.

"Really? You knew all along?" He questioned, confused by my sudden jab at him.

I glanced at him with a half-smile.

"I think I've worked up an appetite, finally, let's go see if your Uncle is at his restaurant so I can question him about how you behave around women.

The look on his face told me some lingering thoughts of that party were dancing in his head. The stabbing thought of how this summer will be entirely different hit me as we walked through the doors of the restaurant and everyone's eyes shifted up to me.

Max introduced me to the owner of 'The Lighthouse' restaurant, his uncle, Ted. He knew who I was before Max introduced us.

In his rough tired tone he spoke as though I were family.

"Dear, if there is anything you want, just let me know."

I thanked him and said some food would be nice.

Max ordered us food from the menu while I hid

myself in a remote booth, trying to avoid the social depression in the diner. Looking around I could feel the same sad and sorry looks that I was tiredly used to. Most people I didn't know, but apparently they knew me. Getting out and coming here was supposed to get my mind off of the reality of my situation. The murmur of whispers at every table here didn't help ease my mind.

I picked through my plate, a club sandwich and onion rings. I wasn't hungry, but forced myself to eat a piece of my sandwich and a few rings. I didn't want Max to see me dismal again today. I think he needed a break from being my babysitter, getting out was an escape for him just as much as it was for me.

When we were finished I told Max I wanted some fresh air, needing to get out of view of gossiping eyes.

I stood outside the lighthouse door, thankful I brought my sweater. It was dark and windy which made the dim lighting eerie. I walked across the wood wharf to where Max and I sat to watch the sunset. The moon was a crescent hanging in the darkness, with no horizon. Somewhere the ocean met the sky, but it was blackness from the edge of the dock to the full moonlit sky.

I heard the door open and close at the restaurant.

"Vi? Where are you?" Max yelled out.

I walked over to him, the wind whipping my hair in my face.

Max nodded to the marina, "Hey, you had mentioned that you didn't want to go home for the night, you don't get motion sick do you? The water sounds rough."

I tried to see which boat Max was pointing at, but of course, I had no idea one from another in the darkness around them.

"Anything is better than home."

The salty air beat at my face making my eyes water, for once the tears not being from my emotional turmoil. I pulled each side of my cardigan, and wrapped it around me tightly.

Max took the lead and directed us to a blue and white sail boat. He took the first step on, and turned, offering me his hand. The dull ocean sounds, the rise and fall of each wave lulled me into calmness. The moon gave off a mellow glow lighting the boat enough to see its main features. Max shifted over to the hatch doors and unlocked them with a key he pulled out from his pocket. I followed his lead once more, down into the dark hole.

"Watch your step, the stairs are steep."

Slowly, I took each step in the pitch dark until Max turned on a lamp. A dull light lit up the insides of his uncle's boat.

The interior of the cabin hung in shadows while my eyes adjusted.

The ladder landed me in the galley, complete with stainless steel appliances spreading the dimness around. The table folded up and hung on the side wall. I peeked around my shoulder and a wooden door showed a dark room further in the front end of the boat, I assumed it was the master bedroom.

In front of me, beyond the table, were two single beds semi confined into the back space. One on each side, Max patted one while a yawn snuck up the back of my throat.

I fell back in the bed, kicking my sneakers to the floor. I passed Max my sweater, and he set it on the kitchen table.

"Are you sure you are ok here?" Max pulled up the blankets, tucking me in.

"Yeah, I'm exhausted."

"Ok. Good, I'm right here if you need me." He leaned in, ducking down, avoiding the low overhang, and kissed my forehead.

"Sleep well Vi."

I fell right to sleep, without having enough time to consider if I could or not. My typical restless sleep wasn't without the accustomed nightmares on the underside of my eyelids. It's like poison seeing every detail of my parents faces whenever I fall asleep, and stabs me every time I reach out in my sleep for their touch.

KISS OF AFFLICTION

CHAPTER 8

I woke up with the sun. Max was still sleeping off the double cheeseburger and fries he inhaled last night, settling him into a good sleep. Sliding on my cold sneakers, and wrapping myself in my soft knit cardigan, I went up to welcome the sun for another day.

Hanging my feet off the front edge of the boat, I sat and got lost in the cold bite of the fresh ocean air. The sun masks and warms me from it. It feeds me something I haven't had in what feels like a long time. Lullabies from the sea grass drawing me in with their dance. And still I lack my previous colorful self.

A rhythmic thudding sound coming closer broke me out of my trance. Realizing they were footsteps, I turned around to see Ted with two black mugs, steam escaping from the top.

"G'day Violet."

I stood up and walked over to where Ted stepped

onto the boat.

"Saw you sittin' out here and thought you might be able to use a coffee, brought one for Max too. He must be still asleep. Brought you the newspaper too. I get them but never read 'em."

He passed the mugs to me, then dug in his pocket and retrieved some packets of sugar.

"I am about to open the restaurant if you want to come on in for breakfast. I can whip up some pretty decent pancakes, or so I am told."

"Thank you Uncle Ted, I can definitely use the coffee. Maybe when Max gets up we will head over for those pancakes. I think I've been depriving him of his meals, he slept like a baby after you fed him."

I sat down on the bench that lined the front side of the boat, sat the mugs down and dumped sugar in each of them. Clinging to my mug with both hands not letting the warmth escape, I turned around and graciously took the paper. I hadn't thought much of the world outside of my own recently.

"Naw, I don't think you are depriving him of much my dear. If he didn't want to be around, he wouldn't be. I am glad he has you. Ever since my brother and his mother got a divorce he could never really find someone to talk to. He has always been closed in that sort of way, and I know Max and your brother were together a lot, so I'm just glad that you have each other."

I sat looking at Ted with a nod of my head agreeing with him. There wasn't much I could say to that. I was very glad Max wanted to be near me.

"Well…" He jumped from the boat to the dock. "Come on in when you need more coffee, I've got more waitin' for ya inside Violet." Turning, he headed for his restaurant.

The coffee was a comforting smell, trumping the scent of the morning dew. It was too hot to drink, but I didn't care, the sun couldn't warm me through the cold morning air and I knew the hot liquid would. I grabbed the newspaper Ted left with no intention on reading it. I usually only ever read the headlines just to check up on the small town news. I unfolded it with the headlining article racing towards me, screaming. "Recent Drunk Driving Kills Parents, Security Boost At Black River High School's Graduation Friday."

A week has passed already. Alex crashed into my parents, killing himself and them. Graduation is in 5 days. How am I supposed to deal with any of this? I froze, I didn't know which thought to process first. Thinking about what happened a week ago was constant, I never forgot.

Graduation. Maybe I would have panicked, maybe I should be. I am totally unprepared for the upcoming initiation. Numbness from the whole situation was creeping in. I could barely handle being in a diner with twenty strangers gawking at me, the graduation ceremony will be much worse. There won't be anybody there to be proud as I accept my diploma. No family to boost the volume of applause at the mention of my name. On that thought, I threw the paper to the floor.

After a few minutes had passed, Max came up from the cabin squinting at me from the brightness of the sun.

"Mornin' Vi." His voice deep and rough from sleep.

"Your Uncle brought us some coffee, yours should still be hot." Coming to sit by me, he took his coffee and started drinking it. No matter what state he is in, he always looks completely collected and thrown together. It gave some people the wrong idea, that he was laid back and didn't care. I knew him well enough to know the difference. His easy going facade balanced me out. He could naturally calm me just by being near.

"Uhhh…Vi? Did a seagull or something attack the newspaper? Why is it blowing all over the boat?"

"Front page article on my parents, it's been a week apparently. They are writing about solutions on drinking for graduation." I took the last gulp of my coffee and sat the mug on a piece of the newspaper so it wouldn't blow anywhere.

"Graduation is on Friday." I informed him. Slowly looking at me with an expression I couldn't read, he went back to his coffee. We sat in our normal silence, with the natural sounds outside our world breaking us from our darkest thoughts.

"Oh, and Ted wants us to go eat breakfast over at The Lighthouse, he's making us pancakes."

Smiling he finished his coffee and hopped up.

"They are a family recipe, want to head over? You didn't eat much last night, you must be hungry." He grabbed my empty mug and looped his finger into both handles.

"I am starting to think you are trying to fatten me up Maxwell. Don't worry so much about me eating, coffee is good. Very, very good."

Before heading over, I took a yellow rain jacket that I found in Ted's boat, and wrapped it around myself to keep the morning chill out of my bones.

Walking slowly down the dock, I looked out to see past the rock barrier surrounding the mouth of the little harbor. Rows of fishing boats were heading out for their morning catch. Seagulls flying far up, following the parade out to sea.

Sitting at the same booth I picked last night, a waitress immediately came over with coffee. I liked her already.

Max gave her our order of pancakes with a side of bacon. He didn't ask me, he just looked at me as if to say 'You better eat it'. I brushed it off, and looked around.

Apparently this little place seems to be a really popular local spot, the cabin style restaurant was very busy. Many people were pitching glances toward us, trying not to make it obvious. I ducked into the corner of the wooden booth, burying myself there. Naturally, I don't like being the center of attention, given the circumstances I can't stand being in the spot light. Especially every time I walk through a door.

Max leaned in over the table. "Vi, they are just worried and feel bad. You can't blame them, your name and picture has been in the newspaper for the past few days."

"It has been? And you didn't tell me?"

"When would I touch on that topic, between your nightmares or the times you stare blankly into space? I'm sorry, but it's really not important."

I looked at him, the old me would be mad at him, but he was right. There are fewer and fewer pieces of the old me left.

"The only reason they get to see that I'm not walking around orphaned or suicidal is because of you. Going back to the boat is starting to sound pretty nice right about now. I don't mind hiding away from people for the rest of my life." I said in almost a whisper across the table.

Getting up from their finished meals, a couple awkwardly approached our secluded booth. The woman was looking down, her forehead creased in a frown, and her hands fidgeted with a straw beach hat. Suddenly I realized her nervousness was caused by me. She hesitated, and then looked up at me. Silence filled our booth. I assumed she'd speak but she stood in front of the table with dread written on her face gawking at me.

"Violet?" She barely croaked.

"Yes?" I was starting to lean back into my corner again. A quick glance at Max told me he was on edge too, waiting to see how I'd react. His sprawled out body started leaning forward towards me with his arms coming out to touch me. He'd know me well enough to know I'd want to run from this situation, but I was cornered.

"Violet, I am Wanda Barington. I worked with your mother at Hallbrook Estates, I was the secretary for her partner at the office. We ate lunch together every week for eleven years."

Again, the stranger looked down. I didn't know what to say. My instinct was to dawn the expected mask I've been wearing and feed her the expected phrases, but instead I retreated to my corner wrapping my sweater around myself seeking any comfort. Max's arm unnaturally stretched across the table lightly rubbing my arm.

"I am so sorry for your losses Violet, I can't begin to assume how you are managing to cope. I just wanted to let you know that everybody in town feels for you and would do anything if they knew what to do. We are all at a loss for words."

"Thank you Mrs. Barington." It was all I could force out, I didn't know what to really say to her honesty.

Reality slapping me in the face for a second time today.

Twenty minutes later, after some effort from Max to get me to talk, I looked up. Max had finished his plate. I ate a little of mine, to maintain Ted's long living pancake reputation. I stuck with what I knew would keep me going, coffee.

The waitress came over and cleared our table. She informed us that the bill was taken care of and to have a nice day.

"Vi, I get it. What you think and how you feel. I get that nobody is in this but us, and nobody will ever understand. You can't take a breath without thoughts of your Mom and Dad, or Alex. I know you don't want to be around anyone, and just want to escape all of this. Everywhere you look, your family is there. I get it."

I looked up to him with angry tears burning my cheeks. I hated the feeling of being sentenced to my own purgatory. While I am among the living, with their regular lives, in their comfortable homes, with families surrounding them. I am mad because I don't want to be in my own skin for even two minutes. So I could get some relief from the weight of everything pressing in on me.

Max shifted from his side of the table, to mine, and blocked any scene our show may have been providing.

"Everybody who thinks they get it has no clue. They feel sorry for me, but I know that they are glad none of this happened to them. Everything I knew is gone and I have no idea how long any of this will even last. I want to run away Max. But really, I have absolutely nothing to run from and nothing to run to. I have nothing left."

Sick and tired of crying, I closed my eyes demanding any tears away.

In a warm, soft voice, Max spoke near my ear with his forehead to my hair. "I haven't left since we met eleven years ago, I haven't left your family, I rarely left your house, and I will never leave you Vi. We both know we need each other. You will never be alone. I know I will never be enough for you, but I will always be right here."

Every word that came out of his mouth sounded more like a promise than comfort. He is torn from the title of blood relative, but is bound to me in just that way. I didn't know what to say, but the beauty is that I don't have to with Max.

"Let's get out of here." He whispered. I wiped my

closed eyes and shook my head.

Driving back out the dirt road I got lost in my many thoughts until Max's cell phone rang it's piercing ring. Max answered it and gave clipped answers to the asked questions on the other end.

"It's my Mom, she says your stuff is still at the house from the past few days, did you want to swing by and grab them?"

"Yeah, sure."

"She said that the lawyer called too, he couldn't get ahold of you at the house so he tried there."

"Oh. Ok."

Knots twisted in my stomach, I didn't know how to feel about what the lawyer would say.

We turned back on to the main road. Going in the direction of his house where I spent the agonizing days after the accident. Aimee, his mother, watched over me during that time, but there was nothing that she could do to truly comfort me. I knew it was hard on her to see me laying in her guest room, comatose for days. Across the hall, Alex locked himself in his bedroom, only coming out when she made him eat or take a shower. I vaguely remember him coming in to sit beside my bed. I didn't move, I felt like I was out of body and physically I wasn't able to acknowledge him, I was still and unwilling. Then he'd be gone again, without a word.

The night before the funeral, hearing Aimee weeping between our open doorways vaguely brought me to consciousness. I had to force myself to remember where I was and why I was there. She tapped on Max's half open door frantically until he came out. His Mom was panicked, speaking in hushed spasms about not knowing what to do and calling the hospital. I slipped in and out of consciousness, only catching key words that'd seep into my mind. Max exploded, bringing me back to a groggy awareness. He closed my door and began to rain anger down on his mother. In the midst of the argument, a bottle crashed to the wood floor. The sharp sound of it shattering made my frail body jump. The smell of hard liquor brought all my senses back, with it all my grief.

The pit of my hollow body heaved. My stomach churned faster with every tainted breath I breathed in. Slowly, my body reacted and I pushed my way out of bed. Dizzy and weak, slamming into the back of the closed door. My hands left my mouth to the doorknob, throwing the door back violently while the hairs on my arms stood in reaction to the pungent smell of whisky hitting my lungs. Running past the two wide eyed faces staring at me, my bare feet were sliced by shards of glass. I stumbled the few feet to the bathroom. Crying and heaving, my shaking arms held my weak body over the toilet bowl.

Max gritted his words out at his drunken mother to get out. He started closing the bathroom door saying, "I'll take care of her and the mess, just go to bed and sleep it off."

Looking out the windshield, the flowers along the highway were starting to bloom. The freshness of summer is everywhere, I can see it, but feel nothing. I used to look at a flower and found simple comfort in it, there is nothing inside to inspire a piece of happiness any more. I'm a wet match without a matchbox, there is no spark or any hope for one.

"Max, why are you doing this to yourself? You've been an awesome babysitter, but I wouldn't blame you if you found your peace with all of this and went on with your summer and graduation."

He was silent, the only noticeable reaction was his tightened grip on the steering wheel.

"Max, you've been picking up my shattered pieces, and I really do appreciate it. Seriously Max, you've got your whole summer, and what about university? It's very selfish of me to keep you from living your life."

"Violet, please shut up. I am here because I need to be, you aren't the one being selfish."

His masked face hinted to smugness with the lack of rebuttal on my end.

I went back to looking out the window mumbling, "I guess we will have to agree to disagree."

KISS OF AFFLICTION

CHAPTER 9

The smell of leather seats and the secretary's strong perfume filled the lawyer's office, even though she wasn't at her desk. We sat in the reception area, waiting.

The secretary, in her white blouse and black skirt walked around the corner carrying a stack of folders.

"Oh, hi Maxwell, are you here to see your father?" Setting the stack of papers down, her eyes cemented on me fidgeting beside Max.

Max's Father earned his partnership with the law firm right before his parents divorced. He left the law firm my parents partnered and accepted the partnership here. Mom always said 'it's just business', but I knew their friendship paid a price for the tactical business move.

The receptionist restlessly toyed with her obviously unnatural blond hair, making sure no loose strands were out of place.

She made me self-conscious. I started wondering if I was at all presentable for being out in public. I haven't looked in a mirror in days. My looks have been the furthest thing in my mind.

Being the literal talk of the town, she gathered herself from the slight shock seeing me gave her. She processed why I had come in.

"Hello Ms. Whitman, I wasn't expecting you in today."

Max answered, "Hi Lorraine. No we aren't here to see Dad. Violet is hoping to see Mr. McArthur if he isn't too busy to squeeze us into his schedule."

'Andrew P. McArthur' is boldly stenciled in black letters on the door facing us. I have never heard of the name until now.

Max grabbed my leg to stop it from wildly bouncing up and down, my nerves trying to find an outlet.

"Sorry." I mumbled.

"When you go in his office, he is just going to go through how to deal with anything that was your parents' property. Like the house."

I put my arms around myself to keep the anxiety building up, locked in.

"What do you mean, when I go in there? You're not making me go in by myself are you? I can't do this alone, Max. I'm not going to understand anything he tells me, and you're good at the technical stuff, you've been around some of it before." My leg randomly picked up where it had left off.

"I didn't know if you'd want me in there, it's a lot of personal information. I don't want you to have to deal with anything alone Vi, I told you, I'm here and I'm not going anywhere. If you want me there, I will be right beside you."

Max put his hand back to the same spot on my leg and left it there, calming me.

Lorraine busied herself at the paper filled desk that sat in front of her. She picked up the receiver to the phone and dialed into the office in front of us asking if we'd be seen before the lawyer went on his lunch. She hung up, and directed her attention back to us.

"Mr. McArthur will see you in about ten minutes, if you don't mind waiting. I've got to run out and do some errands for the office, but he shouldn't be much longer."

With a smile, she picked up her oversized purse and walked out the front door. We sat alone, waiting.

"Vi, you just turned 19 right? On your last birthday?"

Max sat thinking about the legalities of my life, while I wanted to run from them.

"Yeah, I'm 19." I fumbled around with the words in my mouth until they fell out.

Snapshots of my birthday last month started bursting to the forefront of my mind. We had Chinese takeout with its various cartons floating around the dinner table. Mom's amazing chocolate fudge cake was my birthday staple. I looked forward to it every year. Gifts followed our meal in the family room. Alex jumped from behind the couch, landing beside me, throwing a box on my lap in the process.

"You're my favorite sister." He said putting his arm around my shoulders and squeezing hard enough for me to knuckle punch his leg.

"Easy job, since I'm your only sister, you nut!"

I opened his gift and found a braided leather bracelet with a small circular charm near the silver clasps. It was engraved with a V.

"I had to order it to get it just right. Each piece of leather is the favorite color of one of the people in our family. Mine is the black, Mom's is yellow, Dad's is red, Max's is the blue, he's around enough we might as well adopt him, and the violet colored one is, obviously, for you."

For an annoying big brother, he always seems to come through. I turned and hugged him, not knowing what more to do or say. There were no words to tell him how much his gift means to me.

"I don't think I will ever want to take this off. It's perfect!"

I moved my arm toward him trying to hold it in place.

"Can you clasp it for me?"

Max walked in from the dining room with mugs of coffee and handed them out. He bent down beside me, where his book bag sat on the floor, and dug out a wrapped present. The white envelope taped to the top was about the same size as the gift itself. I opened the card and read it to myself.

Alex let out a sigh.

"Dude, do you always need to buy a card that is ten pages long. You know she won't just put it aside for later, she's going to sit here and read the whole damn thing."

I smiled, closing the card, then jabbed Alex in the ribs with my elbow.

"Shut up Alex. It's a really nice card Max, thank you."

I sat the card up on the side table beside the couch, and opened the gift. It was a book, which was pretty obvious even with wrapping paper covering it.

"I thought maybe since your nose is always in a book that you might enjoy some poetry. It's Robert Frost."

"That's awesome! Thanks Max." My hands drifted over the aged cover to the pieces of paper marking some of the pages.

"I hope it's not weird, but it's a first edition with his signature. I figured you'd appreciate something with history to something new. I book marked a few that I liked, just to get you started."

Grinning I flipped through to see the places he suggested.

Alex chuckled beside me. "So not only did you buy her something used, but she's turning you into a book nerd too? Fan-freaking-tastic."

"I love it Max, I'll read them all tonight."

He came over handing me a mug of coffee, sitting on the arm rest beside me.

Mom jumped in on the conversation, a little too enthusiastically.

"Ok, this one is from your Dad and I. It's a birthday and graduation present combined." Mom hauled a big wrapped box from the entryway closet into the family room, and set it in front of me.

I glanced over at Dad who was leaning on the frame of the french doors that divided the family room and the dining room.

I knelt down to the floor, trying to find a way in through the wrapping. Opening up the box, I pulled out a large purple, hard shelled suitcase with a big red bow tied around it.

With a confused look I turned to my mother's beaming face.

Dad, in an almost too quick fashion, spat out, "Look inside."

Inside I picked up an envelope with my name written on it. I pulled out the papers and realized I was holding two plane tickets to Paris.

I was stunned. I read Paris Charles De Gaulle Airport over and over to be sure I wasn't reading it wrong.

"I thought we could have a girls trip to France. You seemed really taken with it all when you did your history report on Paris. What better time then right before you leave us to go to university?"

Mom's grin matched my own. I squealed and threw myself at her, I couldn't hug her enough. At this point we both were jumping up and down together.

After I settled into the thought that I was going to France after graduation, I walked over to my Father and hugged him. Even though he wasn't going, he was obviously happy over my reaction.

"Thanks Dad, this is the best present ever!"

"Hey...!" Alex said throwing a pillow at me. I threw myself on the couch, hugging him.

"The bracelet you gave me is awesome too!" I stretched my arm out looking at it.

"I know it is lil sis, I picked it out! Now, I am excited to see what I get for graduation!"

Mom walked over and messed up his styled hair.

"You'll find out soon enough." Teasing him.

I leaned over and gave Max a hug, "Your gift is awesome too, I really do love it."

He squeezed me back.

"I'm glad you do."

Snapping out of the now, tainted memory, I looked back over to the door with the bold black letters. I had been pulling at the sleeves to my sweater, trying to cover my hands. It suddenly opened.

"Miss Whitmore." He walked out with a warm and inviting tone, the tall man cut in a professional suit extended his hand to shake mine.

I stood to shake his hand. He ushered us into his office where I caught my reflection in a mirror leaning against a wall. I soon realized that I was definitely looking like I'd been hiding in the forest for the last week. Stark contrast to Mr. McArthur's styled suit, which now made me feel uncomfortable with my well-worn, days old, outfit.

"How are you Max? I saw your Father not long ago, he didn't mention that you'd be in today." Max kept close to me. His experience at reading my body language proved to be on point. I pushed down a hard lump in my throat attempting at a little self-control.

"No, my Father didn't know we were coming in. Vi decided coming in today would be best, thanks for taking us without an appointment."

"Don't worry yourself over that, please, have a seat. I have been anticipating your visit. We all have been worried about you Violet, but I see you are in good hands. I wish we could have met under completely different circumstances. We knew each other well, I served on a few committees with them over the years. I am so sorry for your tremendous lost. They were great friends and will be missed."

Withdrawal was becoming my drug of choice, and it was so easy to supply myself with it.

I nodded, not saying anything.

"Well. Let's get to business then. Your parents were really good with keeping their wills revised. Being lawyers themselves, they knew exactly how to avoid complications. This makes it straight forward for you, and easy for me as the executor. So I will go through the technical spiel, just bear with me."

I closed my eyes, and grasped to Max's leg to keep me stable. His arm was fast around my torso, pulling me towards his to lean on. His hand freed mine from his leg and held it weaving his fingers with mine. He was my anchor.

"You aren't alone." Max whispered so softly next to my ear that the lawyer wouldn't have heard.

"Joanna Elizabeth Whitmore and Paul Alexander Whitmore leave their sole dependent, Violet Kathleen Whitmore, the property at 43 Maplehurst Drive in Black River. The contents of said property as part of the estate. The 2009 Lexus GX470 that was in Joanna's name will also go to Violet. The cottage property located on Route Eight in Haverhill, the contents included as part of the estate."

"As for the financial aspect, all accounts in their name will be transferred to you. This includes the savings and checkings accounts, totaling $121,332. RRSPs totaling $198,761....."

The lawyer kept talking about all the finances that are now mine. His mundane words started fusing together in my mind. They had more money than I knew what to do with, and still all I feel is a profound aching sadness.

I hung my head keeping my eyes closed. Focusing on his words was too much, my emotions spilled over onto my cheeks.

"Violet, did you want me to give you a minute?"

Taking a breath I looked up at him.

"No, I'll be alright. It's just a lot to digest."

"These are just formalities dear. I do have some more personal things to discuss and give you as well. I want you to understand that financially, there shouldn't be any burdens for you right now. On top of the two properties and the stocks they invested in which are in a current holdings of $837,800..."

Max piped in as my legal, or emotional, aid.

"Mr. McArthur, I think it's a good idea for Violet and I to have that minute, please?"

"Absolutely. I will go get all the paperwork on Lorraine's desk for Violet to sign.

The executer of my estate, left the room, closing the door behind him. I stared at the papers he left on his desk, with a blank stare. The scene of numbers and letters melting together with the tears pooling in my eyes. Everything that my parents worked for, everything they strived to be, now blotches of ink on recycled paper. I want them, not their money. There is no amount of that could bring me to the place they are.

Our visit progressed, I mechanically got through it. I signed where Max told me to waiting for the moment I could check out. I folded in, the dark couldn't come fast enough. I resigned to the consuming void of darkness, letting it swallow me whole.

KISS OF AFFLICTION

CHAPTER 10

Mom? Dad? Alex?

The sun blazed above them, making it hard to see their silhouettes standing under a big oak tree. Something about the field felt familiar, like warm summer rain or homemade cookies. I started to scan the grassland, seeing more and more things that were so close to familiarity. Turning directly behind me, down a path with two parallel ruts made by tractors coming up and out of the farmland, the scene flooded into place. Gram's old farmhouse sat with white siding brightly shining from the sun. Her field went as far as the eye could see.

The only thing out of place was the oak tree. There wasn't one ever out here, until now. It feels peaceful swaying in the summer air. I sense happiness coming from underneath it where a young Alex sat swinging in a makeshift swing. I only recognized him from photos I had seen him in as a toddler. With every push from Mom, he'd let out a squeal of delight. While Dad, leaning against the thick trunk, watched them with a fond smile.

KISS OF AFFLICTION

Everything is tinted cashmere white, resounding with the same softness. Disappointment seeps into my presence when I noticed that I'm not part of the scene playing out in front of me. I'm waving, mentally drawing them in to catch their attention. The debate festers inside me whether or not to break their moment of happiness, or to be an onlooker as the picture unfolds. It is soothing to just watch them, while slowly walking through the buttercups, giggling to myself every time my little brother squeals.

Slowly, my cozy feeling recedes as fast as the tide that brought it. Interruptions from an abrasive world seep their way into my peace.

The sun descended suddenly under the border beyond. The darkness hung, with my immediate attention to the tree. I frantically began to run, the harder I pushed, the further my family stood. Within seconds an ear splitting clap of thunder hit me. It's lightning lit up the attached cloud hanging widely overheard. I forced myself, running faster than my beating heart could keep up.

Mom and Dad caught me in their gaze, then turned and walked away. Leaving Alex alone swinging in the tree. In the time it took for both cosmos to collide, darkness swallowed the field in its muted pitch. I couldn't see Alex for the darkness. I could feel his panic speaking to me, so I broke my limit of panic and ran towards his fear. Over the hill, moving faster, a set of bright lights came towards my vulnerable brother and Gram's tree. They swerved closer, forming into one solid light and a horn pierced through me with its sharp frantic edge.

"ALEX!!" I bolted upright in my bed, in a panic. Throwing off the blankets covering me, peeling off the layers that kept me away from my family, I trembled with confusion.

Another clap of thunder, with lightning hanging on its shadows, entered my bedroom. The window was open, and the wind was bringing the storm inside. To me.

Max's arms were around me before I could get my feet to the floor to start running after my family. He caught me, bringing my mind back to my bedroom, with the breeze blowing through my window.

"It's ok Vi, it's ok. It was just a bad dream." He spoke like I was fragile and on the verge of breaking.

The adrenaline from my dream, the dark storm in my room, and the added heightened protectiveness of my mind added to the sensation of Max's touch. Before I realized who it was, Max was on the floor with a thud and a groan.

"What the…Vi, it's me, it's ok."

His voice came from beside my bed, out of the sea of black. The lightning struck my nerves again making me jump with its thunderous boom. With the room lit up, I could see a makeshift bed on the floor where Max must have been sleeping. Finally I understood, the storm was outside and everything that made me frantic was just a dream. Max was here for me, sleeping on the floor for my protection.

"Oh! I'm so sorry Max!" Looking down over my bed, I tried following where his voice was coming from.

"My nightmare was so vivid. The lightning scared me awake, but I thought I was still in the dream. Then you touched me and I didn't know it was you. I felt pure fear in my dream, I can still feel it. I'm sorry, are you alright?"

I could hear him moving around on the floor. "It's fine, are you ok?

I could tell he had moved across my bedroom, his silhouette framing the window as a flash of heat lightening persisted in the dark sky. Closing and locking it, another clap of thunder rumbled again. The storm now more subdued with the beating of rain on the window.

He came back over, and sat on the edge of the bed.

"Can I get you anything? You aren't going to do one of your moves and send me back to the floor are you? Because if you do, you will be the one sleeping on the floor tonight." The darkness in the bedroom didn't hide his smirk.

"I am really sorry Max. You became part of a bad hallucination. I promise, no more pushing you on the floor. I didn't hurt you did I?" I grabbed his hand, hoping the terrifying pit of emotions hadn't bled to him.

"Vi, it takes a bit more than a girl pushing me off the bed to hurt me." His normal, sarcastic self, comforted me.

"Oh is that right? Don't tempt me or I may try harder next time."

Silent chuckling came from the edge of my bed and travelled over to me through the mattress. He was hugging me before I had a chance to say or do anything.

"It's nice to hear the old you come back to me, even if

it's for a second or two." My cheek rested on his bare chest. His arms reached across my back and held me tight as if he didn't ever want to let go. He was the warmth my body always needed. An old comfort I wouldn't be able to find anywhere else. I settled into his grip letting myself melt a little. My arms reached around his solid bare torso searching through his closeness, my palms resting on his firm shoulder blades.

After a minute had passed in his arms, I started to process my surroundings. Everything else started to unravel from the last 24 hours. I finished signing my life away at the lawyer's office, then Max drove me home. He told me there were some things he needed to take care of at his house. I decided to stay in my house, hiding myself in my bedroom with the hope that I could keep myself as level as possible in only my room. Exhaustion set in as the sun started to go down and I fell asleep.

"I didn't hear you come in, or make a bed on the floor. That can't be very comfortable." I mumbled into his neck, his arms slowly releasing our hold.

"No, it's not. I think I should take your bed and you sleep down there."

"Nice try, not happening. But you can stay up here with me. I think I sleep better when you are close. Or at least I won't wake up trying to run away from the things in my dreams if your arms are there to remind me where I am."

He grabbed his pillows and a blanket from the floor, and brought them over to my bed. I pushed to one side, and he settled in beside me.

"Better? I wouldn't want to be a bad hostess."

"Yeah, thanks. Wondering though, do you offer your bed to all guys that come knocking on your door?"

Rolling over on my side to face him, I propped my head up on my hand. The window behind him lit everything in the room for a split second with a distant grumble, and I could see the smirk on his face.

"Only to the ones who don't knock." I shot back once the rumble of thunder had passed.

"You might want to stop doing reckless things like that. It's not decent for a good girl like you." His voice was quiet in the darkness, but close and teasing.

"I'd be careful Mr. Gunn, I can throw you back on the floor.

"Mhhmm. Sure you can." The smile didn't fade from Max's smart ass remarks as he lay back and put his arm under my head and pulled me in to rest on his shoulder.

"We better get some more sleep, we have a busy day tomorrow."

"We do?" Bringing my head up to face him, even though it was far too dark to see anything even an inch in front of me.

"Why, what are we doing?"

"Tomorrow is Prom."

"Oh." Putting my head back down in the crook of his

neck in thought.

"Max, I don't care if I go to prom. I have nothing to wear anyway. I don't have tickets. Let's just stay home and order a pizza or something."

"Vi…" His arm was wrapping me into him, pulling me into another hug.

"You've been talking about this for a painfully long time. You will regret not going one day. I don't want to push you to do something you aren't ready to do, but I know deep down this is what you'd want. Even if you don't see it right now."

His words starting to slur together with tiredness, and I let go of the issue as he let go to his sleep. I easily followed, reluctantly drifting into another dream.

I faced a big tree in the middle of a vast field, similar to the one at Gram's in my last nightmare. Even unconscious, the lingering emotions were still forefront of my mind for me to realize this in a dream. The field here was unknown to me, but very refreshing. There was a lightness that wasn't bright, but far from dark. Rows on rows of sun caressed lavender flowed up and down the hills. The dream was so lucid that I could smell the freshness of the purple fragrance. It warmed me to have such a comforting smell in my memory of my mother. She always planted lavender in the flower bed by the porch.

The tree was full of its foliage. The wind brushed the leaves around in the golden sun. To the left of the tree was an old stone structure. Maybe the framework of an abandoned shed. The tree, with its shed, was about fifty feet away from me, but unlike my past dream, I was not anchored to the ground. The tree stood in the exact rocky path that I was following, between the abundant flowers. After wandering along to reach the tree, I sat in the patch of grass and stones at the base of it. The surroundings were a place of ease and admiration, almost like a painting. The natural body of the rocky mountains off in the distance felt whole, bringing me to a new place of myself I had never seen before.

My sleep was peaceful, sitting under the tree among the lavender. I started to wake when the sun shone through my window, welcoming me back to the living. I rubbed my eyes to help stir them awake and realized it was Max's arm my head was still resting on. My motions stirred him, and he turned to me, curling his body around mine.

"Good morning." He whispered in a hoarse morning murmur to the top of my head.

His warmth felt like a hot shower on a cold day, nothing could make me want to leave it.

I could tell he dozed in and out of sleep, his breathing would become heavier for a few minutes, then he'd move his feet around and rub my back with his thumb, and he'd doze off again. His rhythmic breathing almost brought me back to sleep, just before I had, my cell phone rang. Max's arms tensed around me with a complaining moan, and rolled over to answer the annoying sound sitting on the side table.

I ignored the call, I knew today meant Prom, and I was going to ignore that fact until the very last moment. Max's body heat was gone, his arm no longer my pillow, so I tugged at the blankets to pull them up over me. Still talking on the phone, which by now I figured was Kendra planning every detail of the day. Max relaxed back into his spot in my bed. He pulled the blankets up over him and pulled me back into the spot on his shoulder. I wondered if I was acting like a child, his little kid sister needing to be constantly cared for. I pushed the thought out of my head, because I just didn't care. He was safe and warm, and he understood what I needed before I had to ask.

The day went on, with him pulling me out of bed and downstairs for coffee and a bowl of cereal. He brought groceries over last night, anything that was here had expired and had turned bad.

I insisted that we watch a movie on the television, like we'd always find ourselves doing on a day when we had nothing better to do. He reluctantly agreed, ignoring the prep orders Kendra gave him to pass on to me. I promised a shower didn't take as long as she thought it would, but I'd get on my dutiful list as soon as the movie was over. Which I didn't have a chance to try and avoid, he had me upstairs before the credits started touching the television screen at the end of the movie.

Max left me at my bedroom door informing me that he was supposed to leave and meet Kendra at his house thirty minutes ago.

I laughed at him, knowing the impatience she'd lay on him once he showed up.

"Will you be coming back?" I refrained from pouting at him leaving and the end of our lazy day.

"Yeah, I'm going to bring Kendra back with me. She has plans for you, but if you aren't showered and ready for her when we get back, I'm the one who's going to get the heat."

We smiled at each other, because we both knew the truth. Kendra will be like a drill sergeant, and if this evening didn't go as she planned, there will be hell to pay.

"Will you be alright until I get back? I hate leaving you, you know."

"I'm fine Max, you don't need to babysit me. You have a life too you know." I hated that I was lying. I did need him, more than I should. He deserved so much better of his time than dealing with me. One day I will be strong enough to tell him to go live his own life. But that day was not today.

"Call me if you need anything, I won't be long." With a quick kiss on my forehead, he turned with a "See ya." on his lips, and was on his way out.

Turning to my bedroom, I was once again alone. A feeling I kept telling myself I will have to get used to it. I still felt drained, after what feels like weeks of horrible sleep, and an emotional triathlon. The bed looked inviting. I slogged past it, heading into the bathroom to do as I was instructed. Twenty minutes later, I sat in my robe at the vanity in my room, staring at myself.

CHAPTER 11

A mirror only reflects what the owner of the reflection sees, with their heart and mind, not with their eyes. To everyone it is different. It is hard for me to raise my head and see the shell of me, so I turned around and walked to the window ignoring my reflection.

A gentle knock at the door resulted in my best friend walking in without an invitation. It feels like a life time ago that I saw Kendra. Her dress was a light pearl pink with skirts of crinoline filling the door frame. A beaded, strapless bodice, hung on her perfectly. Naturally, she was beautiful. Her blonde hair in lose curls on the top of her head topped off with a dainty sparkling tiara.

Her happiness rubbed off on me seeing her again. She was without the dark flicker of sorrow in her eye that everyone I meet always has. The pity everyone afforded me that I didn't have for sale. She brought my normal with her tonight, and a piece of me lightened in the moment her smile slowly stretched across her face and our eyes met.

"I need help Kendra, I don't know what the heck I'm supposed to be doing here. I'm not at all prepared for this."

I looked a complete mess. My wet hair dripping down past my shoulders, my face as pale as a ghost, and no ambition to get ready for prom. It's the last place I felt like going tonight. Let alone trying to look the part.

"I see that." She came in and turned to close the door.

I could see her taking a side glance at the leftover blankets that made up makeshift bed on the floor. One eye brow rose as she drew her gaze from it to me.

"Having sleepovers?" Kendra teased. With a swoosh of her skirts she walked across my bedroom to the bed.

"Yeah kind of, I'm not sure if you'd call it that. I seem to have less nightmares when he is around. I think he feels sorry for me and feels the responsibility to take Alex's place or something though."

Kendra shifted some bags around that she brought with her, and set them on my bed. Taking a garment bag from the pile, she hooked it on the bathroom door.

Hands on her hips, she turned to me with a look of determination on her face and in her posture.

"Maybe. Or maybe it's something else Vi. You two have been through a lot together. It would be totally natural if something stronger came from it."

I looked at her confused. How could Max and I feel any stronger than we already do, he is the only family I have left.

"Vi, you've never considered the idea that you two were obviously meant to be together. There has been a lot of talk at school about you. Mostly concern, but whispers that you and Max are a couple. I hate to be the one to show you the obvious here, but he's had a thing for you for the last year at least. Did you seriously not know?"

I wasn't sure how to reply, the concept never once entered my mind, and I'm not sure if I wanted it to.

"What? Together as in my boyfriend? He's like a brother, he IS my brother now. That's just weird. He's an awesome guy, and he feels responsible for me, that's all."

"I don't think that's why he is around you all the time Vi. You are right, he is a good guy, with clearly great taste in fashion."

I turned my eyes from his pillow on my bed, up to a short silk dress in a beautiful deep purple that Kendra was unzipping from the black bag, and was holding up for me to see.

"Max handed it to me as soon as we walked in the door, he told me to tell you no more black."

Looking at his choice for me, I reluctantly took it, "What am I supposed to do with this?"

"What do you think Vi? You need to go put it on, and hurry. I obviously need to do something with that mop of hair and add some color to your face."

I walked over and took the hanger the silk fabric hung to.

Kendra hugged me quickly with a sigh. "It's so good to be hanging out with you again Vi. I've missed you."

I patted her back with my free hand. "Missed you too." I said with a slight smile.

The tortured thoughts danced in my head about Max. The dress, prom, his pillow so cozy beside mine.

Kendra butted into my thoughts with her noisy fabrics.

I looked up to her gaze, she was back to business and automatically I gave in. Prematurely, I thought, but I didn't have it in me to argue with her. Not about her theory on Max, or her love for the dress. Max and Kendra both wanted me wearing it, there wasn't much use in arguing against the two of them. The only dress in my closet was the one I wore to the funeral. It is black, with a lot more fabric, obviously not at all what Max was after tonight.

I walked with it to the bathroom and closed the door. I got a better view of his choice. The dress was pretty with spaghetti straps, gathered all through the bodice so that it clung to every inch of the occupant's body. Beautiful? Yes. On me? No. I definitely wouldn't do it justice.

"Uhmm…Kendra, how am I supposed to get into this? It's skin tight!" I cracked open the door to get her advice.

"Vi, I know it's not a pair of jeans, but just get into that dress and get out here. Tic toc, Prom won't wait for us."

Five minutes later, after one minute of squeezing and pulling, another minute of adjusting, and three minutes convincing myself I didn't look ridiculous, I came out.

"Kendra, this is so not my thing." Still adjusting and poking at myself awkwardly.

I looked up in her silence to see her wide smile spread across her face. She sat me down at the vanity without a word. While I was in the bathroom, she set up her makeup kit and had a couple other bags spread out and prepared to tackle the biggest project she will ever attempt. I didn't know what her plan was for me, but she was more prepared for this battle than I was.

I pledged to myself, this will be the only night she gets me to use as her doll.

We've spoken of prom on a weekly basis for about 4 years now. Choosing a dress, then disregarding that one for a new one, repeatedly. Giggling over who we'd go with, never did I think I'd end up with a dress Max picked out and going with him. A lot can change in a short period of time.

"Kendra, should I be scared? What are you about to do to me?"

Staring at me in the mirror with that smile still plastered to her face, she took my hair in her hands.

"Give me about 15 minutes and I will have you ready for Prom." Closing my eyes, I stopped looking at my reflection. A little squeal came from behind me, I assumed the excited squeaks came from her, or the tooth fairy came to collect those dazzling whites that kept popping out from behind that smile.

I sat, quietly, like a good subject. Hair pulled, straightened, sprayed and pulled back. Then she attacked my face, then my eyes. Afterwards, I sighed in relief. I was happy I didn't look like a clown. My makeup was simple but dramatic. I couldn't complain, not that it would matter if I did. While I sat smacking my lips with the lip gloss she shoved in my hand to put on, Kendra started digging through another of her bags. A shoe box appeared and was placed on my bed.

"Max picked out the dress, the shoes were my pick. He told me on the phone yesterday what your dress looked like, mostly because I begged to know. I told him only a girl can pick out the shoes, and to leave that one to me."

"Oh no." My thoughts escaping past my lips. The shoes were 3 inches high, black lace peep toe stilettoes. They were nice, of course. But for me, I wasn't sure if I could even walk in them.

"You want me to wear those and survive the night?"

"Oh it's easy, just walk normally. It's not like you have never worn heals before Vi."

"Yes, heals, not stilts, and not lately."

"Stop being so over dramatic, mine are higher." She mumbled as she bent down past her folds of crinoline and forced my feet into the shoes.

Backing up to the closed bedroom door she waved her hands at me.

"Stand up, let me see."

Feeling like a little girl in a pageant, I stood and walked to the middle of my bedroom. Faced Kendra and stared at her while her eyes raked over me in an inspection.

"Vi, you look amazing!"

Amazing is a strong word for how I felt. I let it go, and told her how much it meant to me for dressing me up like a Barbie doll.

"You know I'd do anything for you Vi. Max is right, you'd regret not going. This might not be how you pictured prom, but I think you are as ready as you can be."

Before I could answer, there was a knock on my door. Kendra squealed again with her broad smile while looking at me, then swung around to answer it. She opened it just enough to tell the intruder to go downstairs and wait. Without a need for a response to her demands, she closed the door before one could be given. A mumbled, "Your date is here." Came through the white door from Max.

"Is that Max? Is he still there? Because I have to give him a piece of my mind." I took two steps toward the door, but she stopped me before I was able to grab ahold of the door handle, and spun me around to face the upright mirror beside the bedroom window.

"Vi, honest, you look awesome! Now, I am going downstairs. Hunter is here and I know he is itching to get going. We are supposed to meet the hockey team at the city gardens for a group picture. Don't touch your makeup or hair, and apply lip gloss as needed. Max said he was taking you, so I am going to get going."

"He did, did he? He seems to have everything figured out tonight."

"Vi, if you need anything, you have my cell number. But we will be meeting you at the school."

"Kendra, this is a lot, but awesome, thanks so much. I've missed you a lot." With a hug she was out the forbidden door, letting the cool air wake up my bedroom.

I turned to look in the full length mirror again, trying to grasp how the reflection looked. I gawked at the purple jewel reflecting back at me. The image just doesn't match what I feel like inside.

The shoes are nice, and after staring for a few minutes, I noticed I was subconsciously tugging at the hem of my dress. Could he have gotten it any shorter?

"WOW!" Max said and exhaled loud enough for me to hear. I turned around to glare at him. He was leaning on the door frame, looking me up and down.

"Vi, you are beautiful!" A little blush catching up to his words colored his cheeks.

"I hear that you picked out this dress, my only problem is, where did you put the bottom half?" I stood, back to the mirror, with my hands on my hips.

Still staring at me he walked halfway across the room with a single red rose in hand. He was in a tux, purple tie to match my dress, and smooth glossy dress shoes.

"Max, are we going to the Prom together?" He

stopped in his tracks, with a crease in his brow.

Of course I knew we were, but I had to give him a touch of the uncomfortable feeling that I was feeling, just to torture him a little.

"I...uh... I just assumed we would go together. If you want to go with me, I didn't know if..."

Smiling I walked over to him and took the rose from his hand. I put it to my nose, it smelled like summer rain.

"I love it. Of course Max, I will go to the prom with you."

With a smile he sat at the foot of my bed. I walked over to the mirror to check out the made over me.

"Are you sure I look alright Max? This dress is skin tight."

"The dress looks better on you than I thought it would, Vi. You are gorgeous."

Coming from him, I couldn't help but blush. He's complimented me before, he's always been very honest with me. But this was different. I was never wearing anything like this, or something he picked out for me.

"Let's go, we need a night out." He stood up, looking at me through the mirror. I turned to him and took the hand that was waiting in the space between us.

My picture perfect date, in his tailored tux and fresh haircut, walked around and opened the passenger side door of his truck. He offered me his hand to help me get up and in the seat. As soon as I took it, it was as though a lightning bolt shot up my arm making my heart race. He must have felt it too because we both were very still and were locked in a fragile stare. There was a moment of confusion, then awkwardness, and I tried desperately to pass it off as anything but what Kendra's suggestions had dripped in to my thoughts.

The drive was quiet, not awkward, but the comfortable quiet that exists between Max and I. The sun was starting to cast its shadows on the night. The easy silence led us both into our own pool of thoughts. Eventually mine ended up in a stabbing heaviness shooting through my chest. Every thought brought me back to my family and how this night should be so different. I tried hard to push it away, and to fight it off. I couldn't do this again to Max or myself. I couldn't ruin this night. It obviously meant so much to Kendra and him, I had to try and push any depressing thoughts aside for them.

Max pulled into the back parking lot at the school. Meant for the school's faculty, somewhat obscured by the trees framing the area on three sides. The school sat in front of us, a little bit in the distance. A paved walkway led from the furthest side of the parking lot to the front door of the school.

I opened my door before Max could get around to it. Directing my knees to face out, trying to search in the darkness for my purse. I never liked the contraptions, leave it to Kendra to stick one in my arm, just to carry one thing.

I held myself up by the dash with one hand, and searched with the other underneath my seat, mumbling obscenities into the shadows of the S.U.V. I was about ready to make the decision to forgo the purse, and the lip gloss inside, when a warm hand slid down the arm that was supporting me at the dash.

"Don't worry about it, I will find it for you."

I held his hand while getting my feet to the ground.

What am I doing? I want to go back to my jeans and hoodie, crawl in bed and burry myself in blankets. I looked up to Max's face, and there with him I felt like I was wrapped in my blankets at home. A feeling that shouldn't leave me wanting or squirming, or confused with the idea of why I now felt this way.

My shoes touched pavement, and I automatically let go of his hand. I took a few steps away from the door, and a couple deep breathes to get my barring.

"Maybe you should have picked out the shoes too Max." Straightening up and placing the dress in all the places I felt were exposed.

"Max? I don't know if I feel up to this attention, maybe we should just go home."

I turned back around to the truck, but he wasn't there. Everything to my right was an empty parking lot until it hit the path that led to the school. I could see the doors wide open with people starting to flow in. We were far enough from them, and in a shadowy corner to not draw any attention to us.

"Max?"

I turned back around to peer into the dark wooded area behind the parking lot. He was there behind the truck, in its shadow, looking at me. Between the dimness of the wooded backdrop and the glow of dusk, his features were dramatically enforced. Tall and built, his facial features carved out by the lights from the parking lot like a Roman bust. If it would have been anybody else, his intense gaze would have made me turn away and run.

As though he could read my mind, the corner of his mouth curved upwards. He had something in his hands and I assumed the smirk was leading into whatever he had planned.

"Max, what are you doing?"

He walked towards me without stopping and took me by my hand. We stopped, standing in front of his four by four where he put his MP3 player into a little cube device giving it speakers, and set it on the hood.

"Well, I wondered if maybe you should take those heels out for a test try before attempting the real deal inside. I want you to remember that we are here for us, together. Not for anybody else. You're not here to put on an act for anybody, it's just you and me, alright?" As he spoke and pulled me gently to him.

A familiar song started playing, I couldn't quite place my mind on what song it was though. I knew that it was one that Alex has played on his guitar. Before I could put much thought into it, Max had a gentle arm around the small of my back, and took my hand in his. We stared at one another, and in the midst of all my thoughts, we started to slowly move to the music. My body naturally responding to the movements Max led.

I think I'm fading away
But I keep thinking that you'll wake me up with a whisper in my ear
I keep hoping that you'll sneak in my room
So I wait and I wait
And I run old scenes through my tired head
Of the days we laid by the school and said forever
Was that the best I'll ever be

Memories flowed out of my eyes and rolled down my cheeks. Max pulled me in tighter without any words, just the song. I put my face into his shoulder and let him carry me through with only the words of the song speaking for the moment.

I miss you
I miss talking all night long with you
And I need this to find a way to your home
My love can you hear me
Have I been hoping loud enough, wishing hard enough
Can you see me when I'm asleep all alone – alone

After what felt like an hour of listening to that one song, our time warping into it, a faint rumble was slowly getting louder. I heard my name being called from the same direction. I couldn't see her through the headlights pointed at us, but I knew it was Kendra. She and her new hockey player boyfriend drove around and parked on the other side of Max's truck.

Max loosened his grip around me, but didn't let go. Before Kendra came over in her whirl of excitement and tulle, I turned my head to look up at Max. He wiped my tears with the pad of his thumb the kissed my forehead. Kendra's voice reached around the vehicles before she had.

"I can't believe this night is finally here! Prom! Can

you believe it Vi?"

All primped and proper in her dress with matching accessories, Kendra left her boyfriend in her trail and ran over to where we were standing hand in hand.

"Uhmm, no... I can't believe it." Plastering a wobbly smile on my face, but she bought it in her haze of happiness. She came closer with her arms out to give me a hug and stopped right in front of us. She looked at me and looked at Max with a scowl.

"Max! What did you do to her?" She pulled me in to her and gave me a hug.

"Vi, come to the car, I have my makeup kit. Let me fix you up, you're makeup is running all over your face."

Scolding me and dragging me at the same time.

After rubbing around my eyes raw with a wet wipe and reapplying my mascara and eyeliner, her face didn't give the smile of shining white pearls as it had before.

"Vi, are you ok? Did we push you into too much too soon?" Her happiness was disappearing and I swore that tonight I wouldn't ruin it for anyone.

I took her arms in my hands.

"No, Max was right, I would have regretted not coming. I just have a lot to sort out and I don't know how or when I will feel more like myself. Maybe I never will. But for tonight, I'm here. Seeing everyone happy makes me happy."

"If you need space or time or anything, just do what you have to do. Don't worry about anybody else but yourself, okay?" I nodded, and her smile returned.

"I've got it, now give me a hug before your hockey guy leaves without you."

Looking back, both guys were standing nodding at Max's S.U.V., with his gaze sliding to me every few seconds. I smiled faintly at him.

"Yeah, Mr. Impatient. I think he is more excited than me!"

"Well then, you are perfect for one another!"

With a quick hug we were off up the parking lot towards the mob of people arriving. The music was coming loud out of the open doors. This was it, I was being thrown back into normal life, and at full force.

KISS OF AFFLICTION

CHAPTER 12

The crowd spilled into the auditorium, which was transformed into a lavish Paris nightline. Complete with a lit up Eiffel Tower and Arc de Triomph. A large realistic looking moon was cropped up over the vast room. Lights twinkled in every direction. In case it wasn't certain what we were looking into, a banner hung from the ceiling with black and gold tulle confirmed the theme of the evening, " La Lune de Paris".

Max was quick to provide the door table with two tickets and soon had his arm around my waist walking inside. We had to make our way through the arranged lobby area, of course losing our social sidekicks in the mob.

As expected, everyone we walked past looked our way with modest glances or bold stares. I didn't feel myself, I've never had this attention before and now wasn't the time I was wanting that light cast on me. I suspect that I am the only girl here that was thinking this way. I pushed it out of my mind, forcing myself forward with a reassuring squeeze on my hip from Max.

Tables were spread out around the dance floor, round discs balanced with center pieces and tableware. The white linens glittered from the gold dusting they were dusted with. Everything was beautifully done.

Max had a hold of my hand and half pulled me along the way to our reserved spot. I could see Kendra sitting at a table ahead of us with a few other assigned guests. I squeezed Max's hand a little tighter in hopes he'd get the message. He squeezed back a few steps before we reached the table. Kendra caught us in her line of vision and started waving her hand for us to join.

"I made sure you were sitting with us. I may, or may not, have switched your place card with Kristen's." Pointing to a table on the other side of the dance floor I could see Kristen and her date sitting at the table, looking very put out and bored. Either she is too bored to be here, but came anyway to be sure she didn't miss anything, or she thought she should come because we deserved her appearance. I've been in school with her since grade one, she is one girl that loves the spot light on her.

"I think you made a wise decision, and I promise not to tell your secret to anyone." Winking at her I walked around to where she was sitting, and took the already stolen seat next to her.

Kendra looked at me then to Max who had assumed his seat beside me.

"Hey Max, would you mind getting Vi and I some punch. I'm all out and I'd love to have some girl chit chat with Vi for a sec."

"Sure." Standing up, he took a step behind my seat, and leaned in to speak over my shoulder.

"When I get back, I'd like to steal you away from the girt talk. I know there are a few people who would love to see you for a minute Vi, if you are ok with that."

"Well, you got me this far, might as well get it done and over with. I surrender." Standing upright, he looked down at me with a grin and put his hand on my shoulder.

"It's about time! I will be right back with your drinks ladies." Then he was gone in the sea of colored dresses and black suits.

Before my gaze was off of Max and back to Kendra, she pummeled me with her suspicions.

"Vi! Is there something between you and Max?"

Shocked, I looked at her not understanding what she meant. Annoyed with me she sighed and leaned in.

"I've been your friend for how long Vi?"

"Since we were in diapers, why?"

"Why haven't you told me about you and Max? Obviously something was going on when we pulled into the parking lot, and he hasn't kept his hands off of you since we've left our car."

"Because there is nothing to tell. He understands what

I'm going through, and I feel the same for him. We are there for each other. I told you, he's just a good guy. He's taking care of me, as much as I hate to admit that I need it."

"I know you've been through hell, and I can't imagine it, not even a little bit. But you and Max, he is completely in deep for you Vi. Whatever has happened in the past couple weeks between you two, whatever it was, he has fallen hard for you. Can't you see that?"

"No, I can't." Feeling a little flushed and confused I looked at Kendra and leaned in as I realized a secret.

"Seriously, nothing has happened between us. He hasn't been any different, neither have I, I don't think. I've wondered why he sticks around, but I think it's because he feels a duty to see me through the way Alex would if he were here." I suddenly fell silent at the idea that Alex would have been to prom tonight with us. At this table. Max would have brought whatever girl he was crushing on, and not me. He has been spending so much time with me, he hasn't had any time to get back to his own life.

"Vi?" Kendra's hand was on my knee.

"Hun do you want to come to the bathroom with me for a breather?"

"Yeah, I think so."

We both headed to the ladies washroom, out the auditorium doors, and into a quiet hallway. There were a few stragglers from the main event out here.

"Hi, Violet." I turned around to see a classmate that I'd hang around with once in a while. If we were in the same class, we'd always partner up. It worked for both of our benefit. I enjoyed the research and she enjoyed doing the presentation in front of the class.

"Oh, hi Emma. Enjoying prom?"

"Isn't it perfect? I was part of the decorating committee and had a blast putting the Paris theme together. How have you been? I've read most of what happened in the newspaper. I'm so sorry I haven't been in touch, I guess I just never knew what to say."

"No, that's ok. I'm, well…I'm here. That's about as good as it gets for right now." I said with a slight smile. Fortunately, she smiled back.

"That's great Violet, I'm glad you came! Well I better get back in there before my date thinks I ran off on him. I'll be in touch ok?"

"Sure!"

Kendra, grabbing my arm, continued on to the washroom.

"Violet, tell me right now, are you going to be ok? With Max, without Max. Here or tomorrow, I don't know what to think. I can see it written all over your face."

Standing in front of the mirrors, her reflection was looking back at me.

"Honestly, I don't know what 'ok' is any more. I can't remember what that feels like. I feel like I've been punched in the gut and I'm clinging to catch my breath. Usually, that's when Max picks me up and pieces me back together."

I started, mindlessly, washing my hands. I suppose the sinks were there in front of us, my body decided to go through the motions.

"I'm finally starting to get ahold of that feeling though, controlling it as best I can."

"Please tell me if there is anything I can do. You're my girl Vi, anything at all just tell me."

I turned to her after drying my hands with the crispy brown paper towel. Taking her hands to divulge an idea I had this morning after the dream of lavender fields.

"Kendra, I do need a bit of help, your aunt is the travel agent downtown isn't she?"

"Yeah, my Aunt Claire."

"Do you remember when my Mom gave me a trip for my birthday? She and I were to go to France. I think I should take that trip, alone. Just to get out of town, out of the house, and figure out what my next step is. I'm feeling claustrophobic in Black River."

"Vi, that is a fantastic idea! Are you sure you should go alone? Maybe Max should go with you. If you left him, I don't think he'd know what to do with himself."

"Kendra, you've got to promise not to say anything to him. I haven't told him yet. I just realized I wanted to go when I found the tickets in my room before you came by to make me Prom worthy. I can't build myself back up if someone else is there doing it for me. Especially now that you think he wants more from me that I just don't think I have. I... I need to be alone in my thoughts, to think. I don't know, seems like all I've been doing is thinking. I need to do something. Plus he needs to do the same, he had a life before all of this and I'm holding him back."

We looked at each other through the reflection of the mirror.

"I don't think he will be happy about your decision. You know Max, big protector, he always has been over you."

"I don't know Ken, but I know I have to go. I have to do this for Mom. I will have to tell him soon, the plane tickets are dated for tomorrow morning."

"Vi! That's almost thrilling, taking off to Paris and only deciding the night before! I will come by in the morning to help with packing and stuff, ok?"

With a chuckle we locked arms and walked out the door, facing the auditorium.

Entering the room we started walking through the graduation class and their dates. There were many passing by leaving a "Hi Violet" hanging in the air. Most I didn't know from which direction or who it came from.

"It's got to be a sign that our theme is Paris, and if it's everything like this, I might not come back." Pointing to the lit up night sky and the cardboard cut outs.

"Well, you better come home, and bring me home something nice." She said with a big smile.

Our table was surrounded, with what appeared to be the entire football team. Catching the direction of their gaze, we saw that they were watching their dates on the dance floor. Kendra walked around the table to Hunter who was talking with another team mate, I assumed. I followed behind her and sat in my chair while she stood with the ogling on lookers.

Noticing a cup of punch that was at my setting on the table, my mind went to Max and where he might have wondered off to. Just as I made the decision to get up and walk around in hopes of finding him, Billy came from behind me and sat in Max's seat, blocking my only exit with his legs.

"Hi, Violet."

The shock, I'm sure, was showing on my face. I've been trying to forget that night for what feels like a long time. I haven't yet dissected the events, how they unfolded, and why I made that call to my brother, while I was supposed to be on a date with him. It was all too much damage control to consider, especially tonight. Here he was, sitting sideways in Max's chair blocking me from getting up, is the face of that night speaking to me.

"Uhm, Hi." I responded while fidgeting with the punch cup.

"I...I've been thinking about you. How are you? I really wanted to apologize for everything that happened on our date."

Shifting my glance from him to the cup of punch to my hem line, to the cup of punch, to my short hem line again. I couldn't look over at him. Why does he need to bring that up now?

He took one of my hands away from my lap and held it.

"Violet, I'm sorry. Is there any way I can make it up to you?"

The anger from my chest was clawing its way up my throat. My hand singed where he was touching it, it felt like fire burning from my temper.

"You are in my seat."

I looked up to see Max, with his hand tense on Billy's shoulder. There was a level of threat to the tone of his low voice that was unmistakable. Not one I've heard before, only heard of.

Billy released my hand back to my care, and picked up the name card with a snide snort.

"So, you are Max Gunn." Tossing it back to its spot on the table, he got up right beside me, wedging himself between Max and I.

"The Max who called me last week?"

I wanted to get up and leave. My throat felt closed off with anger and fear. I could feel Kendra looking at me and back to Max in shock of what was unfolding. I grabbed her hand and held it tight. The guys who were around our table watching the dance floor, were now starting to bring their attention towards us.

Max didn't answer Billy's question, he just stood in his place and stared at him with a frighteningly cold straight face.

"Was it you?" Billy demanded.

The snarl in his voice hinted to many things, his positioning between Max and I hinted to something that made my skin crawl. I could feel it from the pit of my stomach to my throat. The bitterness took me over, it was nothing I've ever felt before. I've met many pieces of myself this past week that I've never known, this boldness washing over me was another to add to the list.

A sound came up my throat, in my voice, but I didn't know what I was saying until it was said. Any mental filter was blown off before I had a chance to control myself.

"Billy." I let go of Kendra's hand, who moved as I got up and took the two steps to be in front of Billy. Max was a few inches from my back, and I stood my ground between them. Both guys over a foot taller than me.

"Look. At. Me." I spat each word at Billy.

Billy broke his gaze with Max to shift it down to me. I stared him in the eye and took a step closer to him, as if he'd be scared of my small frame. Our faces so close they were almost touching.

Slowly I started with my voice seething with pent up anger.

"What I need you to do right now is go. You owe me nothing. You've given me your apology which I accept, only to be done with that night, and of you."

He put his hand up to my waist, lightly enough to touch the silk of my tightly fitted dress.

"I'm not going anywhere, there's more I want to tell you."

Before he had a chance to finish his sentence Max grabbed his jacket with one arm, while pushing me around to his back side. As soon as I was out of the middle, Billy fell to the ground with a punch. I jumped back just in time to not get toppled over from what was spreading out in front of me. I stood in place, trembling with anger, trying to collect myself.

I was torn between trying to handle things myself and Max jumping in to protect me. My anger was throwing fire at my every thought until I screamed at the both of them.

"ENOUGH!" I hadn't recognized my own voice. I stepped to the both of them pushing Max back as hard as I could, and pointed at Billy.

"You! Get up."

I shot my glance back to Max in warning, he knew to control himself with that one glare.

Billy was on his feet, wiping a trickle of blood from his nose.

"You need to leave me alone Billy. I just lost my family, and here you are trying to prove what? I was never yours, and I will never be yours. And trust me, the next time you put your hand on me, it won't be Max protecting me. I am quite able to kick your ass myself. I don't want you near me, I suggest you leave. Now!"

He looked at me then at Max.

I closed my eyes for a split second trying to catch my breath, and rein in my anger. I looked up and Billy was still standing his ground, then smirked and turned to walk away.

I shot another look at Max, "And you! You don't need to jump in every damn time you think I need to be saved! I don't need a God damned babysitter! Alex did the same thing and look where it got him! God! I can take care of myself!"

Billy's voice came from right behind me, "Yeah, she needs a real man!" His arms slithered around my middle to pull my back flush to him.

If it wasn't for my attire, my reaction with this position

would have been much quicker. I had little time to kick off my heels before Max let a growl out of him. In the matter of a second Billy released his clasp and the two guys were throwing punches at one another.

I noticed some of the crowd around us was staring and shouting out at the two guys fighting with one another on the floor beside me.

Panic sinking in at the attention, I looked around until I landed my gaze on Kendra who caught my eyes at the same time. She reached out and grabbed my hand and we ran out to the front door together. I didn't let go of her hand until we reached our parked vehicles.

KISS OF AFFLICTION

CHAPTER 13

Catching our breath we stood in the parking lot, under the light that shone down on us. I tried getting into Max's truck, but of course, it was locked and he had the keys.

Kendra started laughing to herself.

"Vi, when you stood up in front of Billy, you looked like you were the one going to punch him! For a split second I was scared. For him!"

Looking at her, in her princess gown, I couldn't help but laugh with her.

"Here we are in the parking lot, at Prom. With all the planning we've done over the years, this scenario never made the list."

Letting all the tension flow out of me, we were leaning over in laughter. Kendra was trying to catch her breath through the laughing fit.

"Well, to be fair, I didn't plan this dress neither!"

She turned her head to me breaking out in hysterical laughter again.

"No, but seriously Vi, it was made for you. It wouldn't matter what you wore, you always look hot."

I rolled my eyes at her.

"You never see how guys always watch you out of the corner of their eyes! That's what I love about you, you are so naïve, and you just don't care. Look at Billy in there!"

She pointed at the big brick building we just ran out of.

"You may not have picked that dress out, but tonight they are all staring at you, whether you see it or not."

"I'm not sure if this is where I say thank you or go to hell." Smiling we started pulling ourselves together. Kendra went over to Hunter's car to check the locks, luckily it was unlocked, and she was able to secure her makeup bag.

"Hold still, I'm going to give you another touch-up."

While she was trying to fix my eye makeup, which felt more like she was trying to stab me in the eye with her pencils, I couldn't help but wonder what was going on inside.

She must have been reading my thoughts.

"I wonder if we should head back in. I bet they are going to serve dinner soon, I'm starving! I've been busy all day and have barely eaten. There, you are perfect again! I'm just going to go touch up in the car where I have a mirror and some light."

Before she reached the car I saw Max taking long strides down the parking lot towards us, with his jacket flung over his shoulder. I crossed my arms and leaned against the front fender. I wondered if it bugged him that I was touching the paint of his new S.U.V. Just in case it did, I made sure to cover as much surface as I could. Staring him down as he came through the rows of cars.

"Vi, are you ok? I thought maybe something happened to you, that you go hurt or something. I had Kristen check in the bathroom for me in case you were in there. I could have brought you out for air."

"Max, what were you thinking taking Billy down like that? And what is he talking about a call from you? Why would you call Billy? You can't stand Billy!"

He walked around to the passenger door and unlocked it. Holding the door open for me to hop in.

"I'm not leaving Max. I want to know what the hell just happened in there. Then I want to go eat a meal with my friends. You made me wear this dress, I came out in public with it on, I'm not leaving!"

To that he grinned and closed the door.

Kendra piped up from the other side.

"Uh, guys. I think I'm going to head back inside. If it's safe to go back in." Looking at Max for an answer.

"Yeah it's fine."

"Ok, Vi, you good?"

"Yeah, I'm good. We will be in soon."

With that she started back up the school walkway.

I looked back to Max who was leaning against the side of his beauty, obviously not caring if it gets touched. Inwardly, I said damn for that fact. Peeling myself off the fender I walked away from the Jeep in towards the street light, then turned back on him getting ready to hit him with a long rant about how I can take care of myself and he shouldn't feel the need to. That I'm not his responsibility. As I turned he was right in front of me, almost face to face. He started explaining everything to me.

"I called him a few days ago really pissed off over what he did to you. I blamed him for you leaving early and you having to call Alex. I blamed him for it all Vi and I felt really badly for it. So I texted him the day after saying that I knew the accidents weren't his fault and I was really sorry. That I wouldn't apologize for how much hatred I had for him for the way he treated you. I may have told him if he ever touched you again I'd put my fist through his face." He took my hands, searching my face for a reaction, to see if I was mad.

"You call what you just did, an apology? Wow Max,

remind me to never make you mad." I pulled my hands from his and walked out of the light.

"Vi, I'm sorry." I could hear him right on my heels, which were having their own conversation with the pavement.

"I know you are Max," I said as I opened my door to get my purse from somewhere under the seat. I figured after all the effort Kendra has put into my face, I better do her the favour of reapplying my lip gloss. 'As needed'. I heard her directions ringing in my head.

"I just don't understand why you had to attack him in there, I was getting ready to give him a piece of me." Finally dislodging the purse I opened it to be sure the required item was indeed still there.

I felt Max right behind me as he pushed the truck door all the way open. His hand softly ran its way down my left side and rested on my hip I froze while the sensation burned through my body inch by inch giving me goose bumps.

"It was the piece of you that he wanted that set me off. He put his hands on you, and I'm sorry Vi, but if anybody has any piece of you, it's going to be me."

Pushing the goose bumps aside, I started to turn my body around, towards him.

"But Max, I'm going to have to learn to defend myself. You can't swoop in and try to save me all the time. At some point I will need to rely on me. Let's be real, I'm on my own. At some point you need to go and live your life, and I need to be able to let you do that."

His hand didn't move, a small piece of me kept track of where it was, and how his thumb kept moving up and down over my dress. Conflict washed over me with liking the sensation or ignoring it.

We were standing so close I could feel his body heat. I was trying hard not to get locked in his stare, so I kept checking where his tie was coming undone.

Softly speaking I could feel his heart beating through the air between us.

"Violet...he can't have you. Or want you."

"That's because I've got nothing to give, he can't take something that isn't there."

"Vi, listen to what I am trying to tell you." He took his other hand to pull my chin up, forcing me to look into his chocolate brown eyes. "Nobody can have you because what I need, you have, and nobody can take that from me."

Frozen, I couldn't move my body. I couldn't move my eyes from his. His hand was still on my hip regaining what Billy had touched.

"Max..." Finally breaking his stare I looked back down to the tie. My body still wouldn't move, so it was the best I could do to get out of the trance he had me in.

"I don't know what to say. I've got nothing left inside

of me. You, out of anybody, should see that."

I looked up and got trapped in his eyes again, confused at what I was seeing in his face.

"Max, I thought you were just around to pick me up because that is what Alex would have wanted you to do. I thought you were being my fill in big brother until I got my crap together." Searching his face I couldn't make out what he was thinking.

"You're right, it's what Alex would have wanted. At first I owed it to him, to your family, and to you as my friend to see you through this. But Vi, I could have left way before now. When I'm at my Mom's house all I can think about is you. If you are alright, what you are doing, what you are thinking. All I want to do is be with you. That's not what Alex would have wanted me to do." He said with a smirk.

I couldn't help but let that thought touch the corner of my mouth with a grin. My brother would have given him hell for even trying to be closer to me.

"No, I guess it's not."

"Vi, I want you. I always have. Just being your friend has ruined me for other girls. Tonight, I want you more than I ever have."

Stunned by his confessions, he closed the four inches that was between us and kissed my lips softly. Thawing them slowly. They betrayed me and kissed him back. The feeling he was giving me crawled up my spine. A hunger that wanted to release my pent up emotions, but I swallowed it down.

He put his forehead to mine until I could swallow down my shock and move my limbs again. I was able to bring my hand up to his chest, landing over his heart.

"But Max, I'm empty. What if you want me because you want to pick me up every time I fall, you just showed how well you can do that inside. I can't be with someone out of necessity. It has to be because we both equally want each other."

He pulled back a little so we could see each other's face again.

"...and....you don't want me? That kiss told a different story."

"Max." Shaking my head to get myself away from thoughts of the kiss, I shifted a bit to make him lean back.

"I don't even know what I want for lunch, or if I wear clean socks. How can you expect me to know what to love when everything I loved was just ripped away from me a week ago?"

The doors opened up at the school and a whistle came from Hunter with him motioning us to come inside. Kendra probably sent him out to tell us dinner was ready.

When the doors closed again, I stretched over and picked up my purse that was on the seat, and walked out of the way for Max to close the door. I leaned my hip against the fender, getting ready to sigh and pick myself up to brave the crowd.

Faster than my thoughts could react, he grabbed my face gently in his hands and kissed me, not like the one before. He was anxious and hungry in his kiss. Trying to prove a point, trying to show me what he thought I needed to know. Trying to get to the pieces of me that I didn't believe existed any more. I started pulling him away with my hands gently on his chest, to protest his ill concept of what I am and what I have to give him. But that growl came raging up my spine and spread through my body like fire to gasoline. My hollow threats of banging fists on his chest melted in to slithering hands snaking themselves around his waist and pulling him closer to me. Pushing me against the front of the truck, it felt like I was in a cloud of bees buzzing around, the inside world and outside world were like water and oil. Neither could be affected by the other. We were one, his touches and mine equally eager for one another.

Another whistle brought us back. Max pulling his face away, with his hands still holding my face let out a low, throaty growl. The cool air entered our consciousness enough for me to gain some focus.

Clearing my throat, I whispered, "Max..."

"I know what I'm getting into. I've waited a long time to kiss your lips and get under your skin that way. No matter how much you think we aren't meant to be together, you just proved yourself wrong."

Without warning, my hands were around his neck pulling him in for another kiss, meanwhile fighting away the eagerness that dwelled behind it. We stood for a few seconds, with our arms locked on to one another.

"Vi, if we don't go in now, we might as well head home. Right now, I don't care where I am, but my hands are going to have a hard time leaving your skin."

His eyes left mine, and followed his thumb down my jaw, down my neck, drawing invisible lines back and forth on my collar bone.

Slight control kicked in, and I pushed my hands slowly to his chest, and backed off of the truck, pushing his body backwards with mine. I looked up at the school then back up into his face that was looking at me like it had never done before. I slid my arms around him and buried myself in his vest with a hug.

"We better get up there."

I walked a couple steps to grab his jacket, which had been tossed to the center of the hood, and I passed it to him. We rushed up to the auditorium doors, Max flung his jacket over my shoulders, then started fixing his shirt and tie, and buttoning up his vest. I thought at the very least, I could execute plan lip gloss by myself.

By the time we got to the table, the meals had just been served.

"I ordered you both the chicken, but you've missed the first course."

"Thank you Kendra, that was thoughtful of you." Max said as he pulled out my chair for me to sit beside her.

Kendra had her eyes on our every movement, then on me as I tried to look anywhere but at her face. She'd be able to read me like a picture book.

The meal was pretty normal, for once, this evening. Every now and then I'd get a look from Kendra as if to say "What the hell happened?" Everyone at the table made regular grad student chit chat, which pleased me since I didn't have to partake, I just sat back and listened. Max kept his hand on my bare thigh throughout the entire meal. His actions were hidden by the long white linen draped over the table. His fingers would caress the inside of my leg, and I'd glance over at him each time unable to not return his grin. I considered how I didn't see any of this in him before. How quiet he always was when he held me. How blind I obviously am.

As usual, I didn't eat much, but more than usual. Once the dessert and coffee came out, I was happier.

Hunter spoke up, beside Kendra.

"Hey Max, you and Violet should come to Billy's after party. After you both apologized and went your separate ways, he told me to invite you both. He said he knew that if he put his hand on Violet you'd go nuts. And I guess it did eh?"

He looked at me with a big grin and a wink.

"Yup, sure did." I mumbled.

Max pulled his hand off my leg to set it on the back of my chair, lightly brushing his thumb on the nap of my neck. "What do you want to do?"

Kendra piped in saying they were both going and it'd be nice to have her best friend there.

"Yes, fine, I will go." Which left Kendra clapping in excitement.

I leaned in to Max and lowly spoke into his ear, "But I get the next swing at Billy, deal?"

Max chuckled to himself, and pulled my chair closer to him to pull me in so I could lean against him. He kissed me close to my earlobe and whispered very close to my ear.

"No promises."

CHAPTER 14

After the meal, the dance started off with a cheer from the crowd and a loud beat from the DJ. A wave of people surged to the dance floor, taking the hockey team, which always seemed to be around our table, with it. Thankfully. After small talk with most of the team, I was coerced into the promise of a dance with Tyler and Brad, both captains. Brad was captain of the school hockey team and Tyler the captain of the football team. Following the school teams wasn't ever something I was interested in doing, so this was new information to me. The two of them kept throwing out lines at me, one after the other, tripping over themselves for the next impressive line. In the midst of their bragging contest, I threw up my hands in surrender. Between the both of them, they so cleverly, decided that since I committed to a dance with Tyler, it was only fair for the captain of the hockey team, Brad, to have the same privilege.

"If I agree to dancing with the both of you, you need to promise me that neither of you will talk about sports on the dance floor. Oh, and it can't be a fast song neither, I'm not much of a dancer. If I were you, I wouldn't get too excited over dancing with me." I lectured them, half in warning.

Both were standing in front of me, hanging off of one another. Laughing at each other, or me, I couldn't figure out which and shadow of the question twisted on my face.

"Violet, no worries. I've got moves I can teach you." Tyler patted my hand sitting on the table almost sympathetically with a grin.

"Brad, I've seen your moves, the worm isn't classified as a dance move. Plus, I don't think Violet here can manage that in that dress of hers. Maybe you should just stick with dancing with me Violet."

Listening to them was like overhearing our two neighbor's boys walking by. Their conversations were always pointless but a good cause for a laugh. Fortunately, listening to them didn't end up with me on the dance floor.

Shaking my head, I got up from my chair and excused myself.

"Well guys, come find me when you are done tearing it up on the dance floor. I need to go get some fresh air."

"Sure Violet." Brad's face lit up, elbowing Tyler in the ribs.

Tackling each other to the dance floor, they found the two girls they brought, who were obviously enjoying themselves, no cares as to what their dates were doing. Watching all four of them dancing to a heavy bass dance song, and how they bordered a sensual indecency, I was glad only a slow dance was required of me. I could never move my hips like they were, especially not with Brad and Tyler.

In the corner of my eye I caught Kendra on the dance floor with a group of people. She has always been a socialite, knowing everybody. It wasn't hard for everyone to like her in return, she is a ball of charm and energy. Everyone seems to flock towards her.

She gave me a little wave to go out and join her. I shook my head disagreeing with the idea of me swaying around like a giraffe in front of everyone was a good idea.

Everybody that wasn't on the dance floor had gathered in a lounge area under the Arc De Triomph. Max had made his way to the washroom over a few minutes ago and got caught up talking to a few friends who stopped him. Now alone at the table enjoying my solitude, I thought I should take the obligatory march into the deluge of party goers to say my hellos and to answer the highly annoying and persistent question of 'How are you?'

I left my sequined black clutch on my chair and pushed it in. If somebody wants to steal my lip gloss, it's all theirs. They will have Kendra to deal with for their misdemeanor. My patience for carrying it around was extinguished almost as soon as it was in my hands.

Walking around the vacant tables I reached the end of the dance floor, with my back to it, searching through familiar faces to find Max. The crowd was too thick and all I could see were those standing on the outskirts.

Contemplating whether to go and search for Max or head outside, I felt a hand on my shoulder.

"You agreed to a dance, and I'm here to collect, it's a slow dance as requested." Brad gave me a bright white smile and held his hand out for mine.

I looked at him for a moment trying to drum up an exit strategy in my mind. I know I agreed to this, but the whole idea seemed uncomfortable. I needed to come up with something he wouldn't question, but nothing was registering quickly enough. I decided to take one for the team, and took his offered hand.

He walked me out to the center of the floor and we commenced the slow rotation of a slow dance.

"See? This dancing I can manage, just don't throw any other moves in and I will be good until the end of the song."

"What? You wouldn't join me in doing the worm?" He asked in a playful tone with a shocked look on his face.

"Not in a million years Brad. I'd look more like I'm planking than doing the worm."

At that idea, Brad was in stitches laughing at me. His arm stiffened on my back, which my mind automatically took into account and kept tabs on it like a GPS. I silently hoped that my natural instinct won't always be so distrusting of every guy's touch.

"Brad, stop laughing at my inabilities." I playfully slapped his arm, scolding him.

"Violet, all I've been listening to from the girls we brought was how they are such a great dancers. They love to over exaggerate about everything. Here you are, looking better than any other girl here...don't tell them I said that... making me laugh on the dance floor about how awful you are. I wish we would have gotten to know each other better Violet."

The all too familiar gaze glossed over his eyes. I knew something was about to be said to ruin a carefree time.

"I've had a crush on you since the beginning of the school year."

I stopped mid dance, not expecting that. Lately any glossy eyed person who comes my way is offering me sympathies.

I let out a muted, "Oh."

Brad's body urged me to follow, continuing on with our dance. He only got one, and he was determined I'd dance the whole thing with him.

"I don't mean to make this weird, I just had to get it out there. You've been through a lot lately, but just so you know, if you need anything just text or call, and I'm there."

Grabbing me a little more firmly and pulling me in an extra inch he started leading me around the dance floor with a smile on his face trying to lighten the awkward mood our dance took.

"Just follow my lead, I will teach you to dance yet."

I found my voice again, "I never said I was awful, just that I'm not good." I said with a smirk.

The song came to an end soon after his confession, and we were back to our starting point.

"Well, I guess I know how to dance then, and I've got you to thank." I took his hand with a smile, and we shook on a job well done.

"Will you be at Billy's after party? I can give you your second dance lesson there."

Brad's date came up to him and put her arm around his waist and clung to him in a territorial way. She whispered something in his ear and glanced at me.

"Yeah I will be there, might have to take a rain check on the lesson though. See you there."

Before it felt any more awkward, I turned and walked away towards the doors. I walked along the outskirts of the Arc congregation, and pushed my way to the entrance not seeing Max.

The outside air was crisp. It felt so nice to have some fresh air in my lungs, and to have some quiet. The sky was withdrawn and dark, and as June weather goes on the east coast, always cool in the evenings. Granted, I've barely got anything covering me, and the thought of a jacket completely slipped my mind.

Soon, I found myself wandering away from the

school, to get a better view of the stars, and yes, to be a loner for a few minutes. I followed the path leading to the football field. I had never really been here before, and after last night's rain my heels were sinking into the soft ground. The steel bleachers gave off a glow from the light of the moon, so I decided to head there to save my shoes. As soon as the first metallic clank came from my feet, I heard someone clearing their throat as if to say something. My gaze followed the direction of the noise and I barely saw a figure sitting there.

The unknown person broke the silence, "Hey Violet."

There was no doubt who's voice was that deep and husky. Mason Jenkins sat at the end of the bleachers drawing in on a cigarette, lighting the red cherry in the blackness.

Mason was another friend of Alex and Max's, he'd been over to the house several times to hang out, mostly working on Alex's car.

"Oh, hey Mason. Sorry, I didn't mean to intrude. I was just looking for some place quiet."

"Wow, darlin', you clean up good! Especially for Alex's kid sister." He teased heartedly as if it were any given day, in any given situation.

"Thanks. I think." I awkwardly let out, a sigh escaping my lips.

The reality of his words sobering his now close face, until his head slumped down away from my gaze.

"Do you mind if I sit? I'm not staying long, I just needed to get away for a bit. It's a bit suffocating in there."

"Yeah, of course." He patted beside him, the metal bleacher giving off a hollow metal sound.

He sat up and took off his black tux jacket. His hand slipped in his suit jacket, and pulled out his pack of cigarettes. He patted the seat next to him once more, as I sat he put the jacket over my shoulders with a squeeze. The raw emotion of his lost friend still written on his darkened face.

"Thanks Mason." I managed a small smile.

He leaned back, putting his thoughts behind his eyes. "I hope you don't mind if I smoke. I came out for fresh air too." With his dry sarcasm he lit up another cigarette and blew the smoke away from me.

We sat, and stared at the night sky. It was dark all around the field, only the few stars trickled their light down just enough to be able to see the shapes around the field. It's nice to be around someone who appreciates the quiet, without feeling the need to make it into something it's not. That's one of the reasons why I enjoy being around Max. We sat like this for a while. I'd close my eyes from time to time forcing my mind on nothing but emptiness. It was safe and more than I could ask from myself, but I pushed for nothingness. I forced my inner self to start the brickwork for the walls I needed to survive tonight, and the future.

Mason shifted in his spot and threw his half smoked

cigarette to the ground. His arms stretched along the bench behind us as he leaned back, looking up into the night sky.

"I miss him. Alex. I know that is stupid, me telling you that of all people."

"No, it's not stupid." I opened my eyes to look at him, then switched up to where he was focused.

"I guess it reminds me that I'm not alone." I whimpered, choking a sob on the last word.

He turned his head to look at me, but I didn't take my eyes off the sky. He took something out of his vest, and handed me the full ornamented flask.

"It's better than what they are serving in there." He nodded toward the big brick building behind us.

I took it with no other thought than the night sky and Alex up there watching over me.

The smooth crude liquid choked me as I swallowed it down. Its flames licking my throat, hugging me as it went down and churned in my stomach. I chugged until my body rejected the idea, pushing through the bite in my throat and its fire in my belly.

We passed the flask back and forth in our silence as the clouds moved out and the moon lit the field.

I took one last chug, and passed it back to him. He made quick work of the last of it.

Clearing my throat to get my words past the burn.

"Thanks Mason, thanks for being a good friend."

He chuckled.

"All I did was give you whiskey."

"Yup, and that's good enough for now."

Mason lit up another cigarette with the flicker of his lighter. This drew the attention of someone walking by the fenced entrance of the field.

"Mason, is that you?" A female voice slightly demanded the question.

"Yeah Sara, I'm over here. Just having a smoke."

"Hey Mason, is Violet with you? I can't find her."

With a jolly twist to his words, Mason jeered at Max, "Ah!! Max! Lost your date so early in the night, eh buddy? She's smoking hot, no shock she left your sorry ass for someone else."

I punched Mason in the arm for teasing. With a surprised laugh and a 'Hey!!', he rubbed his arm, cigarette hanging from his lips.

"I'm over here Max, taking advantage of Mason apparently." I rolled my eyes, nobody able to see in the dark night.

Mason's girlfriend stomped over the wet field in her heels, not at all impressed. My suggestion not helping the situation any.

"Is that so? And who do you think you are?" Putting her corsaged hand on her hip, where her tightly fitting red dress clung.

I looked at Mason who just shrugged his shoulders and took a puff on his cigarette. A little giggle bubbled up my throat. I looked up at her looming over me.

"Relax, relax, this stud muffin is all yours." I tapped his leg.

"I just came out for some fresh air." Standing up, apparently too fast, I tried to get a hold of the lightness in my head.

I heard footsteps coming up the bleachers and Max's hand held my elbow and pulled me to him. Leaning on him made standing much easier.

"Jesus Mason, what'd you do to her?"

Picking up the empty flask from the bleacher and shaking it.

"We were just catching up. Don't worry Gunn, we were just blowing off some steam."

I looked down at his groomed hairy face and shaggy hair. Mason gave me a quick wink and went back to his cigarette. It was an understood acknowledgement that we shared that connection, no matter the level. It was in us, we wished for Alex to be here. On these bleachers, raising hell as he always did. It was here that I was going to make sure that Alex would be celebrated tonight.

Interrupting the ache in my heart, Mason's territorial girlfriend wedged herself between him and me, sitting in my vacated spot.

Max slid Mason's jacket off my shoulders and handed it to him. An annoyed sigh came from beside him, when Mason slid his jacket back on, not offering it to his lovely lady of the night.

"Sorry dear, did you want my jacket?" Mason asked her.

"No. What I want is to go back inside where everybody else is having fun." She pouted

"We'll go in once I'm finished up here. Won't be long."

"Yeah, that's what you said when you came outside."

Max and I took our queue, taking my hand helping me down the metal steps. Woozy in the shoes Kendra thought were such a fantastic idea.

Once I got back on the ground, I turned to see the red cherry burning brightly from where his silhouette sat.

"See ya around Mason."

"See ya kid."

And I turned and started walking across the field, as functional as possible with my heels perforating the field once again.

CHAPTER 15

Max had his jacket around me in no time and we started up the pathway with his arm around my waist for support.

"Can you walk straight?" He said distantly.

I stopped walking and looked at him.

"Max, I'm not drunk! I only had a bit of whiskey for crying out loud. Have you not seen the shoes you are trying to kill me in?"

"Vi, you wreak of whiskey, it's reeling off your breath. You shouldn't go back inside like that." His voice sounded too controlled and suppressed.

"Oh. Yeah, I don't have any gum or mints." I felt a pang of embarrassment, which I shoved down. I have no reason to feel embarrassed for something I wanted to do.

"People are starting to go anyway, meeting at Billy's

Dad's yacht for the party. Maybe we should just head home."

"It's on a yacht?"

"Yeah." He said factually, a bit cooler than his usual tone with me.

I started forward, following the pathway to the left where it forked, going to the parking lot.

"Well, we better go. We told everyone we would."

Max caught up to me, and had his arm around my waist where it's been making itself at home tonight. We walked to his truck, listening to excited shouts and cars starting. He unlocked my door then turned to me. He almost looked mad at me, which wasn't something I was at all used to. Not from him. Without a word he picked me up, tucking his arm under my legs, and set me on my seat. Grabbing my buckle he leaned over and gently buckled me in. Staying within inches in front of my face, he turned his eyes to mine.

"Vi, you drinking... it scares me and I really don't like it. It's not who you are."

I scoffed. Who I was, who I am, who I am supposed to be, who is this person? I bit my lip so I wouldn't push my words at him, not wanting to make him any more angry with me.

A sigh came through his lips, and I noticed the slightest sag in his shoulders.

"The last time I let someone I cared for drink, he did something really stupid and left a lot of crap for us to figure out. I love Alex like a brother and the pain stabs me constantly with him gone. But you, you… Vi, I need you. I can handle pain, I am handling pain. But it hurts on a whole different level to see you in pain. If that is why you want to drink…"

My breathing became shallow with the rhythm of my heart beat picking up. The swirls of whiskey dancing in my unexperienced head. Any brain signals from my brain to my body were stunned.

My eyes were locked onto his, not blinking as my shyness begged them to. There was no more sounds of cars, no more laughter, anything beyond us in this moment faded from the Earth.

"I'm not saying don't drink. But if it's something you are going to do, just make sure I'm around ok? I need to be there if you were to do something stupid, I refuse let anything bad happen to you."

Max's gaze was so forceful, like he was pleading with my soul, burrowing into my heart. I could feel his warm breath on my mouth when he spoke, fuelling the whiskey. I couldn't answer him, speech was not an option. We both blame ourselves for Alex. I couldn't make sense if his pleading. If it was to protect his own guilt or something different.

My reliable, trustworthy thoughts were surrendering to the confusing smog behind my eyes and I couldn't connect to them, or them to me.

Without thought, or permission, my hands slowly raised up and stroked Max's hair, feeling his soft waves in between my fingers. I understood his hurt. I didn't want to, but it's what was left of Alex being gone. I didn't want Max in pain, and being with him makes it less agonizing. Gently I pulled his head closer to mine and kissed him softly. Taking me by surprise, one of his hands came up and grasped the side of my neck. His touch ignited the growing electricity burning from him to me, and back again. The softness of what was only meant to be a comfort became something hungry. Something I didn't understand, and I pulled back from his lips breathing heavily.

He put his forehead to mine, rubbing my jawline with his thumb.

"Vi, promise me." He whispered, half pained.

"Ok." I mouthed, barely audible.

I slowly gathered my thoughts, Max's thumb still tracing my jaw made it difficult. He kept his forehead to mine, feeling something that I didn't want to break with my own movements.

"Max, Mason and I started talking about Alex, and I guess it was just a reason to drink. But I'm not my brother, and I most certainly wouldn't drive. And I can take care of myself, nothing bad is going to happen to me."

He pulled his head away from mine, looking in thought.

"I'm not saying I am going to drink and I'm not saying I won't. Who I was is irrelevant; I don't know who I am anymore. But tonight, I'm just going with the flow, if this is how the people who knew him are going to honor him, then I want to be part of it. With his friends, with his stories, with whiskey, with my pain, with whatever I can do to be close to him tonight. It's all I have left. You and I, we are going to celebrate his life tonight. Because you are the only one who is going to understand why I have to do this." I grabbed his head with both my hands to make him see what I was after.

He looked at me, his thumb stilled at my neck to my touch.

Frustrated with myself I continued on, "I don't know what to say any more, I can't want to sit home and sleep days at a time. I can't escape anything in my head, I need to do something."

My hands fell back down to my lap, and I closed my eyes pushing down the ball of tears rising in my throat.

"If he's really looking down, I don't think he'd be happy to see what I'm about to do with his little sister." His finger caught my chin to pull my face back up to his. I opened my eyes, confused. Max smirked looking at me, his eyes scorching into mine.

Max took my head in his hands, and kissed my forehead, lingering long enough to jump start my pulse. He left trails of kisses from there to my eyelids, my cheek, to my neck and collar bone. Then up to my lips, and kissed me with no reservation. He was taking everything he had wanted to. Our breathing became faster, my fingers pulled at his hair as I, unthinkingly, was taking what he was giving.

He pulled back, biting his bottom lip, his eyes following his thumb on my bottom lip. As if it were hard to do, he pulled away and stepped back to close my door. My neck still screamed where his hands were, wanting them back. I blushed over the thought, and bit my bottom lip trying not to smile foolishly.

Max drove out of the parking lot, following the continuously moving lineup of cars heading in the same direction.

"Can we stop at home for a minute. I need to freshen up. Plus, we should grab a bottle of wine from the liquor cabinet, we can bring it with us. We probably shouldn't arrive empty handed. Well, I guess…I wouldn't know, I've never been to a party that didn't have balloons and require a wrapped present."

"Why don't we stay in my Uncle's boat tonight, I can give him a quick call to make sure that it's alright. It's right by the Yacht Club so we wouldn't have to take a taxi home."

"Yeah, okay, but I want my pillow and blankets this time. I'm not complaining, but a little warmth and comfort wouldn't hurt."

It was about eleven o'clock when we drove up the

pier and parked in front of where Ted's boat stays docked. The dim boat lights were already on so we could see our way. I hadn't noticed before, the painted name on the side. In big dark calligraphy letters it was written 'The Twisted Anchor'. I scoffed to myself, you and me both.

Tossing the bags toward the cabin door, Max walked over to the door and opened it. The light washed up over the deck of the boat. He turned to me, holding his hand out so I could come on board.

"Uncle Ted must have come down and turned the lights on for us. Want to pass me the bags and pillows, I will just throw them in here." He was making his way down the few stairs into the belly of the beast.

Passing everything down to him, I took off my shoes and tossed them down hearing "Hey, OW!" and a laugh which spread a grin across my face.

I turned around and followed them down, which took all of six steps. I turned and was really able to see everything for the first time. The last time we were in I didn't take note of anything.

"I had no idea it was this nice in here! I might not want to leave."

Looking at me, he grinned. "I just had the best view I've ever seen from this boat."

"I can still kick your ass Gunn, don't push me." I threw a pillow at him.

Max had been quiet the whole drive down, and still

was reserved to his own thoughts. I walked over to one of the beds that were still unmade from when we were here a couple nights ago.

"Max, you've been pretty quiet since we left the school. Are you ok?"

He sat across from me on the other bed and looked at the wood floor for a few seconds. He still looked well put together in his suit. Taking a deep breath, he rubbed his face, exhaled, and looked at me.

"Just a lot of thoughts about Alex are popping up tonight. I'll be fine. How about we get to Billy's party."

"Oh yeah, I almost forgot the wine, did you remember it?"

He looked at me for a millisecond too long, which made it slightly awkward.

"I brought a bottle of champagne instead. You said you wanted to toast to Alex, plus it's easier on the head come morning. The first night you drink shouldn't be whiskey."

He fetched it out of my backpack and handed the bottle to me.

"Who says I've never had a few drinks before?" I raised an eyebrow questioning him.

He smiled shaking his head.

Unconsciously, we stood at the exact same time. The

space between the beds was barely enough room for us both, I almost lost my balance and was about to fall back down. Max caught me around my waist, and I held fast onto the bottle of champagne so it didn't drop to the hardwood floors.

"Cramped quarters." I said holding him with my one available arm. "Saved the champagne though."

"Violet, you seem to have found more ways in one evening to hold me to you than you've ever in the past. You better be careful, I might get the wrong idea." Squinting my eyes to assess his now smug expression, he seized me around my back giving my balance a push in the way gravity was trying to take me. Falling to the velvet like mattress behind me, with him on top of me, the champagne bottle hitting the mattress with a thud.

"You are quite full of yourself tonight Max." I couldn't help a half smile.

"Are you complaining Vi?"

"Yes! Every time you touch me...I can't think! Like now, you are making it very hard to use function of my brain... Stop looking at me like that!" I tried to wriggle out from under him and out of his arms but it was obviously pointless, especially in this dress. He had me pinned.

He slowly bent down and trailed kisses up the left side of my neck, "Then maybe you need to stop thinking, and definitely stop squirming like that. It has quite the same brain numbing effect on me."

Mentally struggling, I tried hard to remember why I should fight him.

He slowly brushed my lips with his and followed with kisses down the right side of my neck. Paralyzing me in the process.

"Maybe you need to stop battling for control, and let me take care of you."

Moving slowly to my ear, whispering slowly, "Because I know you know you want me, too."

All logical thinking ceased with his breath on my ear. Only one question was clear, did I want to be with Max?

It felt like a struggle to recoil from his attempts when they felt this good. Slowly my lips started to thaw and move slowly.

"How can you want to be with me?"

He shifted his body weight some, and slowly pulled back.

"How can I want to be with you? I don't know if I should be mad at you for thinking so little about yourself or hold you for sounding so small. You are beautiful, a total nerd, you do little things that make me laugh. There are so many times I can't keep my eyes off of you because you hypnotize me. And there are so many times I have to physically force myself not to touch you, but I crave your touch so much."

I bit my bottom lip and pushed some of the hair out

of my face with the one free hand I had available.

"Vi, I'm serious. There is something about you that draws me in like an ache. I always want to be touching you, protecting you, seeing you smile or laugh. I've never felt like this before." His voice was soft, and the honesty in his eyes was a direct line to my heavy beating heart.

"Max, I'm not trying to make you want me. If there is something I've done to make you think I am your answer, I never meant to. I just... I don't know who I am or what I am anymore." I tried to break eye contact, looking at something else would help me regain some function of my thoughts.

A stillness crept into the quiet ocean air.

He searched my face and all I could say was, "I think we are going to be late to the party."

He kissed my forehead and got up holding his hand out to help me get vertical. I went up the stairs first, with him only two steps behind.

"This is one of those moments I can't keep my eyes off you Vi." He snickered to himself.

"Max!" I sped up the last steps and sat along the bench seats to put my shoes on. Max put his jacket around me, then ran his fingers through his flawless wavy hair. He helped me step over the boat, and we walked down the wharf arm in arm.

The Yacht club wasn't far down the wharf. All the boats tie up at the same pier, the sail boats cluster together on one side, the side Ted's boat and restaurant are on. Down the wharf, on the other side, boasts a big nautical themed wooden building and the yachts are tied down around it.

Walking closer, passing a cascade of increasingly larger boats, it was obvious which boat was Billy's parents. Every inch was lit up with lights and people were strewn everywhere. The music could be heard almost as far as where The Twisted Anchor was docked.

We waded through the people on the dock, and found our way on board. Alex held my hand, and even when I tried to let it drop, he gave a slight squeeze. I'd look back to see him grin at me.

I thought the second level would give a better vantage point to find Kendra. I directed us through the bodies of people, and stopped at the bottom of the stairs. I turned to throw a glare at Max.

I tried to let go of his hand, but his entwined fingers held mine in place.

"You can go first this time, I don't need you checking me out again, thank you."

"Vi, and I'm only saying this to protect your virtue here, everybody else will be checking you out and getting a free show, if I don't go up behind you."

Finding it hard to argue his point, and I so badly wanted to, I sighed heavily annoyed with everything. The dress, the stairs, the wandering eyes, and with Max's cocky charm. I turned to go up the stairs. Max's hand slipped away from mine, and slid its way to my waist. He stayed close to protect, what he considered to be, my virtue.

We walked around the loop on the top deck looking for Kendra on both levels, but couldn't find her. Around the last turn a dark and empty area caught my eye. I went to it, with Max catching my idea before I spoke it. We took over the corner section where a built in sofa curved the back section of the upper deck. I sat the bottle of champagne on the glass cocktail table in front of us and kicked my shoes to the corner by Max's feet. The coolness of the deck floor was more than welcomed against my aching feet. This was probably the only calm spot on the whole boat, which was perfect for me.

Looking around, I spotted a bar with a curved counter, topped with inventory for a bar. I pulled myself up to stand, my feet reveling over the feel of the flat surface. Max's hand trailed down my arm from where he had been freely tracing his thumb up and down the crook of my neck.

His fingers tightened at my wrist, which did unexpected things to my pulse. I looked back and took him all in.

"I'm not running away, just going over there."

He sat in the corner of the white leather sofa with his other arm sprawled across the back. Looking at him you'd think he owned the boat the way his posture seeped in possession, relaxed and controlled. Catching his assuming smirk, my wandering gaze must have given me away as to where my mind was going. Stopping at his mouth, I got caught up in his heart stopping smile.

"See something you like?"

I bit my lip trying to hide the stupid grin trying to spread across my face. Seeing Max like this, with me, it was near too much. It drugged me, making me lose all sense. I tried as best as I could to push the feeling away, but my smile still teased at my lips.

Bringing my hand up to his lips, he lightly brushed a kiss over my knuckles. He looked up, scorching my mind with his heavy lidded gaze. The seconds slowed, with the blood pumping through my body, threatening to catch on fire. His voice husky and low, overdosing me with his words.

"Baby, I'm never letting you go."

CHAPTER 16

I stood in front of him, awkwardly gawking at his insanely ridiculous hot body owning the boat, owning my hand, and completely enrapturing my body. I didn't move. I couldn't.

My inner voice scolded me for enjoying him so much, completely ruining the moment.

He slowly released my hand, placing his arm in the same position as his other. I hesitated on a pivot, and stumbled feeling high on him. Filling my lungs with ocean air, I mentally controlled each step forward and stood near the door to the upper cabin. Feeling his eyes on me, I intuitively looked his way catching back up in his heated gaze. Reacting, I tore myself away not letting myself get caught up in the moment. I knew that what he wanted, I couldn't give. I'm not enough for what he deserves.

I reached out and shakily grabbed two wine glasses

that were hanging upside down by a wire holder. I slid them out. I caught sight of a cork screw, figuring we'd need it. I grabbed it and returned to where I was sitting, repeatedly telling myself not to look directly at Max again.

"I think we need a drink." I said grabbing the green bottle from the table beside me.

I handed the bottle and cork screw to Max, my hands a little unsteady to attempt the job. He looked at me considering something, and took both.

"Let's toast to Alex." I shot my head in the direction of Kendra's voice. Her blond curls and light colored dress coming towards us with her bright smile shinning at me in the darkness. She sat beside me and put her arm around my shoulders, kissing my hair.

"You ok?" She asked softly.

I gave her a weak smile and shook my head.

Max got up and walked over to get another glass for Kendra. He returned back, his confident stride not deterred by my awkwardness near him. He poured us each a glass, and handed them to us. Hi fingers brushing against mine in the transfer. Our eyes caught for a second too long, my body craving more of him. I broke the pull, taking my eyes to my wine glass now in my hands, over my lap.

"To Alex, He is missed but always with us." Max said for our three person party.

The charge in the air changed instantly, and Max

raised his glass. Kendra clinked it with an endearing look on her face, from Max to me. I held mine up, and they both touched mine with theirs at the same time. We drank to that solemn thought. He is missed.

I tucked my feet up under me and leaned my head back to find Max's arm there. My thoughts were drug into memories of Alex, and I stared at the stars wondering if Alex and my parents were really up there looking down. I couldn't deny Max's touch, as much as I wanted to. It was my only solace in the world. Greedily I accepted his nudge to lean in on him.

Kendra poured more champagne in our glasses, the first hadn't lasted long as we made small talk about prom and the stories she had heard in the women's bathroom.

As we sat, our private party became more and more populated with friends of Max's and friends of Kendra sitting and standing around us.

Kendra leaned in to Max and I.

"So, why aren't we downstairs dancing the night away?"

"Because I don't dance, take your shoes off and stay here with us." I poured her what was left of the bottle and shoved it in her hand.

By now, many people were following the flow up the stairs and into the second story that used to be a private party. I spotted Brad and Tyler who were playing with a hidden panel on the wall by the small bar. The music started blaring out of the surround speakers all around the deck, and the upstairs was now swallowed by the expanding party from below.

I looked up to Max, my movements beginning to feel lose. He broke from his conversation with the few guys sitting beside him to look at me.

I flushed at having all his attention, and barely got out what I wanted to say.

"There goes our quiet party."

He brushed the crook of my neck claiming my racing heart with his touch. His arm never left me no matter how we sat or stood. He grinned at me and kissed my hairline saying nothing with words, but I knew the meaning. Our time together could be anything anywhere. It was exhausting trying to not be selfish with him, but I was, I knew I was. He wasn't for me to have like this. I was taking and not giving, and at some point I had to be the one who was strong enough to know that I wasn't enough.

"Violet!" Tyler and Brad yelled in unison, breaking my troubled thoughts. They were waving at me, exchanging some words between themselves. Tyler walked our way while Brad disappeared downstairs. I untucked myself from Max's sheltering wing and sat up. Tyler was tall and broad across the shoulders. He strode over to our corner of the boat, white dress shirt, tie and vest, making him easy on the eyes. His hair scooped across his forehead in a single angled flow.

He stood a few feet in front of Kendra and I. Kendra

was engaged in a conversation with Kristen.

"Hey Kendra, where's Hunter?"

She turned to answer him, remembering how long she had been up here.

"I lost him downstairs dancing a while ago." She took the last sip of her champagne and set the glass on the table in front of us. "I should probably go look for him on the dance floor down stairs. That's probably where he is."

She giggled and stood up, looking at me.

"Want to come dance with me? Please?"

Before I could tell her what she already knew, I'd embarrass her if I even tried, Tyler broke her question.

"Speaking of dancing, you disappeared from Prom before I could get that dance you promised me Violet. Are you able to honour me with your presence down on the dance floor? Brad tells me you have some pretty awesome moves."

Max's arm had slowly made its way from behind my head to my waist once I had sat up to speak to Tyler. His hand resting on my waist had tightened. I glanced at him, he was still talking to the guys beside him not giving Tyler much attention, but obviously he had heard the question.

Tyler held his hand out over the table to join him, oblivious to the body language I was getting from my date. I leaned down and grabbed my shoes from the floor, breaking Max's hold on me. I slid them on and grabbed my glass, polishing off the mouthful of the bubbly.

"Won't be long." I said to Max, putting my hand on his leg to get up. Then pushed by him to get around the table. My hand slid into Tyler's as he led me down the stairs. His hand gave me the added support I needed to face the stairs after the champagne and whiskey induced warmth that spread through my limbs.

Kendra was halfway down the staircase looking out over at the dancing crowd below. She turned and smiled at me, grabbing my other hand as we passed by her and followed us down. Tyler led us through a very dense crowd of people until we came up to what seemed like the entire hockey team. Kendra finally seeing Hunter, let go of my hand. I caught her before she passed by me and hugged her.

"Come back and get me in 5 minutes ok?" With a squeeze she pulled back with her blinding smile and shook her head. Then she trailed off to him, throwing her arms around his shoulders and hitching her body on his in an almost indecent dance move. The guys around them all let out whoops as she and Hunter carried on to the beat of the song.

I leaned in to Tyler, the music so loud I had to get uncomfortably close to his face.

"Tyler, the terms of the agreement was a slow dance. There is no way I can dance to this."

Letting go of my hand he walked over to a little sectioned off DJ station and spoke to the bored looking hired hand.

Tyler turned back to me, the upbeat tempo steering straight into a slow dance without a pause.

He placed one of my hands around his neck, and the other he held with his hand holding it firmly. Slowly, we started dancing along with all the other couples on the dance floor.

"English class hasn't been the same without you the last couple weeks." He said almost talking to my forehead. I had to tilt my head up to try and understand what he meant.

"What do you mean? Why wouldn't English class be any different than any other time?" A sliver of a smirk on his face eased the edge of my confusion.

With a smug smile he gave a half eye roll.

"We actually had to do the work, there wasn't any one there eager to throw her hand up to answer Mr. Thorn's probing questions."

"Aahhh.." is what came out when realization hit me. A snide remark strummed at my hateful alter ego hissing, 'That must suck that you had to answer questions while I was burying my family.' I pushed it aside, tonight I'm just going with the flow trying hard not to think about anything.

"Plus I missed you being my eye candy." He dipped me, with a little squeak coming out of me.

"My moves aren't that good!" I scorned him with a slap to his hard bicep.

"Your brother and I, we hung out a few times." Tyler continued mid thought. He grunted as though he was trying to choke down a laugh.

"Yeah, I asked him once if it was cool to ask you out. He made it very clear it wasn't." He gave another snort in remembrance. "He was cool though, I mean just...he was real. He'd give it to you straight up. It's hard to find people who speak their mind to your face you know?"

"Yeah." I swallowed, hard. "I know."

Tyler looked down at me, I refused to look up knowing I'd feel fragile and cry. He stopped dancing and yelled over my shoulder to Brad.

"Hey, Brad! Get us some shots!" In no time Brad was back with a handful of clear purple looking shots. Tyler took two, and shoved one in my hand.

"Let's toast to Alex!" Both Brad and Tyler shouted out so the others around us would quiet down and join in. I saw different kinds of shot glasses, cans of beer, and a variety of drinks going around until everyone was holding something.

"To Alex…" Tyler spoke, holding his arm hooked around my waist. In unison the crowd repeated and everyone took a drink. I felt like a lurker watching them in a ritual I didn't understand. Then all of a sudden, a bunch of people behind our immediate circle yelled out, "To

Alex." One voice lingered and said "you fucker!" I smiled with tears streaming down my face, and drank the shot that was in my hand.

It was sickeningly sweet, and made my stomach churn, but I didn't care.

I caught many faces looking at me, in the middle of the expanding circle, tears sliding down my cheeks. Their eyes reminding me I wasn't a lurker after all. I was part of this, but all their eyes made me uncomfortable. Brad handed me another of the same shot. I raised it while everyone's eyes were still trained on my tear stained face.

"To my brother." I lost my voice and edge on the last word. Stopping to let a sob escape, I closed my eyes to gain some backbone. I took a deep breath without opening my eyes and continued.

"The fucker!" I pushed the words as loud as I could get them out, but barely audible over the hum of the crowd and music.

I tipped my head back and let the burning sweetness slide down my throat once more. I wiped my tears away, and opened my eyes. Everyone was solemnly still, but taking a drink to my unconventional speech. Then it seemed, all at once, everyone was hugging me, smiling, laughing, and letting out whoops.

Kendra pushed through the crowd and gave me a tight squeeze.

"If you need to get away, I'm right here. Just say the

words and I will clear the floor for us to go."

I looked at her, as she wiped the drying tears away.

"I'm ok, maybe another shot?" She smiled, and nodded, then headed back through the thick party happening around us.

Tyler soon had me moving on the dance floor again.

"So Violet, what's with you and Max? Are you guys dating?"

"Nothing like beating around the bush, eh Tyler?" I smiled up at him. "Uhmm…No, not really. I don't really know. It's complicated. I'm complicated."

The song stopped and another picked up, a little faster, but nothing like the fast one Kendra was grinding on Tyler to earlier. Its smooth transition was just like before, no break between songs. Unfortunately, not giving me a guided moment to break our hold and politely leave.

"Well if you aren't dating him then maybe you should put yourself out in the world so I could ask you out on a date."

I looked up at him thinking he was kidding.

"Didn't you bring a date? Tyler, you aren't really asking me out when you have a date here with you, are you?"

Then I felt his arms go from my lower back where I figured was my safe zone, sliding slowly downwards. His smile getting wider in his devilish way.

"Maybe I am."

I stopped dancing and swatted at his arm, "Tyler!"

"I'm cutting in." Max's voice was dry behind me, no hint of a question

I could feel his stare on my dance partner from over my shoulder. Tyler slowing his movements, was trying to decide whether to object or oblige the intrusion. He was eyeing what I knew was a controlled face behind me. Waiting a second too long to decide, Max stepped to my side holding his hand out.

"Sure." Tyler looked at me and smiled, "See you soon Violet." Then disappeared into the crowd that surrounded us.

Kendra popped up by my other side with another shot in hand. She leaned close to my ear, out of hearing range of Max.

"Here. I could see where that was going. He's had his eyes on you all night, and by he, I mean the both of them." She clinked my shot glass and we downed the pink liquid.

An arm from behind me seared its way around my lower torso. Only Max's touch made me squirm guiltily, I didn't have to look behind to check that it was him. My body already knew.

I pushed another little glass of the pink sweet liquid down, pushing my thoughts down with it. I turned to set the glass on a table two feet away. Turning, Max handed me a glass that was empty except some melted ice cubes. It smelled like whiskey. I took his queue, setting it down.

He had left his jacket upstairs, and had his tie and top button undone on his dress shirt. His sleeves were rolled up his arms, giving him a very relaxed look. His face was lit up with different colors from the lights of the dance floor. A smile smoothed over his face, the kind that I couldn't help reciprocating. Taking a step closer he slid one of his arms around my lower back to bring me closer.

"Vi, can I have this dance? You know, we didn't get to dance at Prom. You will dance with anyone, but you didn't save a dance for me." Sounding dramatically hurt and upset, he put on a playful pout on his lips.

The song had a steady heavy beat, not one I'd choose to dance to. My body started swaying with his, hips to hips moving in the same direction at the same time.

Staring at his face I noticed his tongue licking his bottom lip. I bit my own, grabbing at any other thought but his tongue, there.

"Play nice. You get me all the time, didn't your mother ever teach you to share?"

The corner of his mouth twisted up in a smirk.

My movements feeling fluid with the alcohol in my blood, and the movements of his body against mine.

"Vi, you know I'm not willing to share you with anyone. And I don't play nice." His low raspy voice and his heavy gaze peering down at me made my body follow his rhythm, until we ended up dancing alongside Kendra and Hunter. She looked over and grinned her toothy white smile and let out a scream when the intoxicating beat started for Summer by Calvin Harris. We had listened to this for the past month while prepping for Prom. She was yelling the lyrics, barely audible for the volume of the song. I giggled and started to loosen my grip on Max. He pulled me in tight and moved, my body automatically following him. I didn't know how I was moving to the music, I could never hold a beat to save my life.

My movements fed off of his, even through the near raunchy hip movements he guided mine through. His smile induced my own. His forehead rested on mine with our sweaty bodies tuned as one. His mouth so close to mine I could taste the hot air from his breathing. My body begged for more. My mouth reacting selfishly, it took his and let his eagerness melt into mine.

KISS OF AFFLICTION

CHAPTER 17

A few shouts from the hockey team clustered nearby broke my heady fog. I broke my mouth from his slowly, his teeth catching my bottom lip before I could pull away. He kissed me once more, this time more of a show since he knew people were watching.

The song blended back into something slower. Max kissed my forehead and grabbed my hand, entwining his fingers with mine.

We stopped at a table covered with filled drinks for the taking. Max handed me a cup with beer and took one for himself.

Kendra startled me, running up to my side with far too much enthusiasm. The energy from the dance floor seeping away from the reality of what we just did.

"Oh good, your dance is done! Come with me!" She

giggled as she drug me through the crowd to the bow of the boat. Hunter and a few people were sitting with their legs hanging over the sides, drinks in one hand, and a cigar in the other.

The openness in this narrow spot of the boat allowed the cool night air to wake my feverish body. I made quick work of my beer, it was cool and my body welcomed anything cooling it off.

On the way across the yacht, Kendra must have grabbed another round of shots. She shoved one in my hand, and one in Max's, and handed the other to Hunter.

This one was not like the others. It wasn't sweet or thick. It was clear and burned all the way down throwing me into a coughing fit. Max rubbed my back with a chuckle once he saw I was fine.

"Ok, no more of those!" I told her in between coughs.

Max and Hunter were in a conversation by the time I was able to breath straight again.

Kendra smiled and wrapped her arms around me. Again.

"I'm going to miss you when you are in Paris eating croissants and baguettes. Shopping in all those French boutiques!"

Stiffening in her grasp, I suddenly felt sick. I could sense Max's intense stare from a few feet away. I didn't have to look at him, I knew he heard her, I could feel the weight anchoring me to him.

The boat was spinning, no matter how hard I pushed my eyelids closed to focus on nothing. I opened my eyes and caught Max leaning against the railing beside me, looking blankly into my face.

"Paris? What does she mean?" his voice muted and blunt.

Kendra lessened her grasp on me from my other side and withdrew slowly. We caught eyes after she pulled back far enough for her to mouth 'so sorry'.

I couldn't answer him, I ran over to the far railing where it was dark and nobody lingered, and let go of my tormented stomach. I tried pushing Max at arm's length when he came up beside me. My stomach clenched and I heaved, tormenting my thoughts. Max held my hair until tears rolled down my cheeks and I was shivering. When I looked at him, his face was chiseled into a mask. I couldn't tell what he was thinking.

Kendra at my side once more, dabbed my forehead with a wet towel, wiping under my eyes afterwards to fix my sweat and tear soaked makeup.

She spoke up, "Don't look now, but Billy's walking our way." A dry heave wrenched my stomach seconds before he was close.

"Hey guys, why didn't you come find me when you got here! I've been waiting for you to show up. Hey, sorry about before Max, I was just messin' around. I probably shouldn't have taken it so far." He handed Max a bottle of beer as a peace offering. Then handed one to me, Max taking it in his free hand.

"I just wanted to say sorry, no hard feelings."

"Right. Thanks for the beer." Max said in a cool tone. Billy nodded and carried on with the guests as he walked back down the boat.

Max handed the full bottles to Kendra.

"I think it's time we leave."

"Ok" I said limply.

Kendra was soon over to hug me again. She spoke really softly in my ear, "I will call you tomorrow, if you need anything tonight, just call. I'm really sorry, I shouldn't have said anything with Max so near."

Nodding, I pulled out of our hug to leave. Her gaze set from me to Max, then back again.

Max held me around my waist, his hand clutched to my hip, and I gladly leaned on his solid warm body shivering. I tucked my arm around his back for added support. His normal embrace feeling lack lustered at the thought of him being upset with me.

Max guided me to the wooden marina, holding me tightly so I didn't trip over myself. The night air brought me out of my dizziness and calmed my stomach enough to realize Max was too quiet.

He held me as we walked along to the sandy beach running parallel to the wooden pier. I took off my shoes, which had automatically sank into the wet sand, and hooked them on one finger. It was dark, but the moon lit up the water well enough to see in front of us. Walking on the wet sand felt nice, a steady rhythm seemed to wake my thoughts up enough to wonder what the point of drinking like that was. Why did everybody enjoy drinking to the point of power puking? Remembering how I danced with Max flashed brightly in my mind. I moaned inwardly.

A frown played on my face, looking out at the dark water.

Cutting through the contemplation of my thoughts, Max sharply inhaled and was curt with the question built up inside him.

"Vi, why was Kendra talking about Paris? Are you going?" He faced into the darkness in front of us, not looking at me.

I swallowed hard, pushing myself to get the words past my lips and tell him.

I was impressed that my steps didn't falter with my thoughts. My subconscious finally kicked in and drunkenly swayed about wondering why the hell was I so afraid to tell him, it's not at all his decision to make, it's my own.

"I'm going to go on the trip Mom bought me for my birthday. Getting away for a couple weeks to clear my head seems like a good idea."

He stopped in his tracks, grabbing my arm so I'd stop along with him. He stood at my side, and I kept my range of view away from his face. I could feel his turned glare on me. I kept my focus on Ted's restaurant in the distance.

"You are planning to go to France? When?" His words had a controlled hardness that drained any remaining alcohol affect, sobering my mind entirely. I knew he wouldn't be impressed by my decision, but it made me angry at the thought he wouldn't approve. I decided I was going with or without his approval. It was better for him in the long run anyway.

This is where I need to find strength for the both of us, I told myself.

I struggled at the idea of hurting him, especially after tonight. Leaving him may mean more to him than it had just this morning.

I swallowed hard, nothing in my throat to push down but my anger and guilt. I turned to him and gave him the truth, whether he really wanted to hear the answer or not.

"The ticket is dated for tomorrow, and I doubt I can get it changed..."

He let go of me and stalked three steps ahead, stopped, and turned facing me. I could see the shadows playing in his mind, his face set to mine. I saw the information processing through his face as he took a step then stopped. His voice lost the previous resigned control.

"TOMORROW? You are leaving for France tomorrow? When were you planning on tell me? Were you even going to tell me?"

His hands pushed through his hair, trying to push back his temper. His arms came down with a loud sigh from his lips, and curled up into fists, not knowing what to do with his frustration.

"Max, stop over reacting." I couldn't rein in my annoyance with him. "The tickets were bought for me to go. Why wouldn't I? That's what Mom would have wanted." I started walking in the direction we were destined for, passing him and his stone set face along the way. The cold was creeping up my spine, and chills left me cold from the inside out. I assumed it was the chill in the air and not Max's anger towards me.

"Dammit Vi!" I heard him pivot in the sand, and caught up to my side. He followed me silently to his Uncle's boat, his irritation vibrating off of him.

It was silent until we got in to the cabin of the boat. I was furious. I kept playing the situation on repeat in my head. Kendra, my best friend, thought it was such a great idea. Max is supposed to be my best friend too, why couldn't he see it the same way? He poking at the idea of being my old self again, to be happy again, he should be the first person to understand.

Max closed the door at the top of the stairs and stepped down the last step into the galley. He stayed at the bottom of the stairs not turning around, holding on to the railing with white knuckles trying to hold something back. His other hand ran through his hair as if he wanted to say something but didn't know how to. I stood waiting, my eyes on his white shirt that rippled with his rigidity. He was completely silent, but I could tell his breathing was accelerated which told me his thoughts were everywhere.

Injecting calm into my voice, I forced my words out.

"Max, after being best friends for so long, why don't you see I need you to be alright with my decision. I need this, you have told me how I need to start living again. I want to find my old self more than anything, I just need some time. I don't know of any other way." I looked down to my twisted leather bracelet Alex had given me, my hands twisting, and playing with it nervously.

His head started bobbing up and down as if in agreeance with something I said. Turning slowly, I could see a half smile on his face, but it was hollow.

"You're right Vi, why wouldn't I be happy?"

He paused, his reaction whipping my anger to the forefront in defense.

He gazed at me.

"You aren't the only one hurting you know, but I don't run away from my problems. That's exactly what you are doing, running away from your life. I stay, I face my fears, I deal with the crap that's been piled our way. Is it me? Do you want to get away from me? It's hard not to think that right now!"

Kicking me in the gut with the coldness in his words. The blood rushed to my head once again and the cabin started spinning. I pushed the idea of throwing up aside because my anger was starting to feel much stronger than any alcohol playing with the leftovers in my stomach.

"Holy crap Max, listen to yourself! I have been

attached to you for the past week, how is that running? I've done nothing to be accused of that. Yes, after tonight I am completely confused about you and I, but why would I go to Paris to avoid you? You want the old me back more than anyone, and yet you don't want to let her be just that. I don't know who I am any more, but I do know this, the way you kiss me, you are kissing the old Violet, not who I am now. I don't even remember what it is to be her anymore!"

I let out an exasperated sigh and threw my shoes at the floor.

"Everybody freaking waited until Alex died, and now they decide it's a free for all to be with me. For what? I'm a complete mess!"

I turned to him with my hands on my hips, shock sliding over his face.

"It's so easy now that I don't have a big brother standing in the way. Is that why you are all into me now? Is that why you'd risk our friendship? Was it too tempting for you now that he isn't here? God!!"

Looking around I felt like heading back up to the top of the boat, but couldn't because Max was standing at the bottom of the steps.

"You don't owe Alex anything Max! You've been a great babysitter, but I will never have a big brother again and you can't fill his place. You can't fight every guy that wants to date me, the way he did. Is that why you want me, just to claim your territory to warn off the crazies? You can't protect me the way he did, he's gone and I need to do that for myself. I should have done it on my own anyway, but I never had the fucking choice!"

Max's body shifted, pulling his weight off of the chrome ladder, to his feet.

"Violet! You are so...argh… You're blind! I haven't been around this last week because I thought I owed something to Alex! That is stupid and seriously puts me down to a very base level in your life. Do you honestly think I have been taking care of you, or that I am around just to keep guys away from you because that is what Alex would want?"

Before he could prove me otherwise I threw his answer back at him, my voice louder than I expected it to be.

"Of course! You've never wanted to date me before now, but all of a sudden you are going to be my knight in shining armor coming in on your high horse and rescue me from my grief? Now that I actually have guys around you are keeping them away. Do I want them? No, of course I don't, but you aren't even giving me a chance to tell them so!"

I looked him in the face, not understanding why he bothers with me.

Bringing my volume down, I asked the obvious question. "So why then? Why waste your time on me like this Max? You could have had a great time tonight with some blond drooling over you. That's exactly what you should have done. Get on with your life and not worry over me. I will figure all this crap out, I promise you I will, but you need to stop making me want you."

He uncrossed his arms, his eyes softening, and walked over to the sink. Standing there, resting his hip against the counter, he looked at my face with deep thought coursing behind his brooding eyes.

"I've always thought about you and I being together Vi, that can't be a huge shock to you. I've never been great at hiding it. But Alex always threatened everyone who came near you, and I guess I never knew how to approach him about you, but I was working myself up to asking you to Prom. I know how stupid that sounds. I know now, more than ever, how short life is. These are things you'd know if you'd stop and just consider it. I know I love you Vi."

His last words were slowly whispered.

"Especially tonight, I know I don't need anything more than how I want you. You make everything better just by being in my life. I'm ruined without you, I already know that without question."

He took a step toward me with his pleading gaze set on my face.

I held my hand up to stop him from coming further. I couldn't digest any of what he had been trying hard to confess.

"That's just it Max, why would we push what we

already have? It would be irreversible and entirely based on grief and necessity at this point. If not for the fact that we understand each other so much with everything we've been going through, would you still want me? Would you still need me then? Would I?"

Exhaustion set in, heavy on my shoulders. Arguing with him after today's experiences was draining and frustrating. I pulled away from his stare as best I could. Undoing my hair from the tight pony tail, I shook it out, and stood up to open the window near the master bedroom door. The only cure for my unease and discomfort was the fresh ocean air. The round window opened, after unlocking the latch, and eased out catching on the hinge half way. My hand rested on the wall beside the release of air coming in over my face, and I stilled, letting my body relax a little.

Standing right behind me, Max's voice was deep and raspy.

"I guess we will never know what would have happened. Too much has happened between us since then, but I know on every level, everything boils down to the fact that without you, there is nothing in this world for me."

My body was hyper aware of his close presence. Without a touch to my skin, my flesh crawled in goose bumps and the briefest thought of wrapping my arms around his body and kissing him stabbed at the inside of my closed eyes. I stayed still afraid of my body betraying my logical thoughts.

I heard the lightest shuffle of his pants as he took a step towards me, his fingertips grazing over the fabric of my dress, following the lines of my hips.

"I want you to stay here with me Vi, don't run away from me."

Even if I could run, he had me cornered, my body temperature climbing despite the cool breeze grazing over my skin.

I controlled myself and spoke at the window.

"Max, you had a life, one that you were excited about. That wasn't my life. I wasn't on that path that you were destined to take. I have no family any more, Max. No one. I don't know whether I'm coming or going. I'm not running away. My mother wanted me to travel, she wanted me to experience life and that is what I want to try and do. If not for myself, then for her." My voice faltered on the last part of my speech.

Without feeling him, I could tell his body tensed at the idea of me not giving him what he wanted. The stabbing guilt crowded my boldness. Taking my hand off the wall, I regained my balance and turned. His face was inches from mine, anchoring the pull between us.

"I'm not leaving you Max. I will be back in two weeks. I wish I wasn't empty, for you. I wish I could give you that so much. You deserve so much more than me. I'm a shell of a life that no longer exists. I need to try and pick up my own pieces. I appreciate you more than I can ever tell you. You've been here for me, but no matter how shattered I am, I am alone and the sooner I face that reality the better it is for the both of us."

Trying to control the tears brimming in my eyes, they traitorously escaped down my cheeks. Max's anguish was written on his face, grabbing me and clasping onto my body trying to sooth me with his closeness. My body welcomed his, wrapping itself around his, the natural way it always seemed to do. It's always a war between my body and my mind when it comes to his touch.

Gritting through his teeth, his warm breath touched my ear.

"You. Are not. Alone."

A sob escaped through my mouth, misleading my side of the argument. I nudged out of his arms, sliding around him to gain some distance. Just the thought of his touch, made my brain fog up far too easily. I forced my legs, and walked to the landing at the base of the metal ladder.

I summoned as much strength as I could to regain my frustration towards him, keeping us on track. I clenched the rail, with my back to him as he had done to me a few short minutes ago.

"I am alone. You need to stop believing that we can live happily ever after Max. You are supposed to go to university. What do I do then? Follow you?"

I could tell from where his voice came from, he hadn't moved.

"Is it that hard to picture yourself with me?" His strained words twisted into me, making my heart hurt even more, if that were even possible.

He let out a familiar sigh, I knew he was shoving his hands through his hair, frustrated with me. Lately, it was always because of me.

"I haven't thought about university Vi, you have been my only thought lately. The last thing I want to do is leave town."

I remembered all the movies from when I was young, when the kid had to release an animal they had cared for because it was the best thing for their companion. Their best friend. It was a lesson of selflessness.

Love. I do love Max. I do. I always have, but is it contorted enough to give Max what he is needing from me?

I turned and set an attempted glazed look on him with my arms folding in front of me.

"See, that's where we differ. I HAVE to leave. I can't stay here and see everyone's commiseration written all over their faces. I have no choice but to be reminded every time I drive by where the accident was, the mall, everybody from school! Everything is a horrifying memory here. I can't sit and plan the future, I can't carry hope in my pocket for one day when I'll be able to use it. All I have is today, Maybe tomorrow. I have to go. You are not sentenced to my future."

I had started pacing, mid-sentence, trying to drill into his concrete skull why me leaving was an even better idea now, than it was an hour ago. Trying to strengthen my case towards him. Pleading with him to understand, and if not that, than to just agree.

Stopping, I took a deep breath and leaned back against the galley counter starting to feel exhaustion creep back in. I couldn't physically or emotionally argue with him anymore. I looked over at him, my shoulders feeling the curve of submission. My body was giving in, it had no more fight left.

Max was staring at me anxiously. His face looked closed off and defensive.

I let out a low breath to steady myself. I knew what he needed me to say, and I was giving him the opposite, disappointing him in so many ways.

I broke our tense silence.

"Max, it's not that I don't love you."

I looked down quickly to find more words to better explain.

"You know that I do, I always have. And yes, I need you too and I guess I can see how you've needed me in that. But that is my point, I've been totally selfish with how much you obviously love me."

He looked at me in that piercing way when he tries to read me from the outside in, as if he were the only one to hold the key.

"Max, don't look at me like that. I don't know how to love, not the kind that you deserve. Not the kind where all of the world falls away and all I can see is you. The kind where my heart aches for only you. I want to, God I want to, but my heart aches in all the wrong ways right now. I don't know if I will ever be able to twist that ache into something good. Good enough for you."

I looked down allowing the tears to fall without restraining them. I had no restraint left tonight. My strength has been spent.

Taking the few steps to cross the cabin, he buried me in his chest. His hands searched out mine, entwining his fingers between my own.

He set his forehead down to mine, forcing me to look directly into his melting brown eyes.

"I think the question is, would've you wanted to be with me before all of this happened? When I was just Max, and you were just Vi."

KISS OF AFFLICTION

CHAPTER 18

The direct and obviousness of his question struck me, blowing a barred, gated area wide open in my mind. All of our moments together since childhood, everything flashed on the backs of my closed eye lids at warp speed. The way he'd look at me across the gazebo when I was reading and we'd smile, and I'd suppress a giggle. Holding the door open for me when we'd all shuffle into Mom's S.U.V. and him sitting beside me with his arm stretched behind my headrest every time. The time he got his new truck and I was the first person he called to go for a ride in it. He always was at the passenger door to open it when he'd pick me up for school, putting his hand on the small of my back to guide me in. Giving me honest answers when I asked him to, and the way he lied to me to save my feelings from getting hurt. The pureness in those moments never faded, obviously.

I always compared Max and Alex as the same in their actions whenever something was mentioned about me dating, or another guy wanting to take me out. In my mind

Max always mirrored Alex's reactions. His look was always a disapproving one in that situation. He'd always remind me that there was other fish in the sea, not to hop at the first bottom feeder. He always seemed tense, telling me any guy would never be good enough. A total brother move in my mind.

My mouth was dry, and I was stunned at the answer forming in my head. Perspective on every moment, from small to huge, shifted to a different angle in one second of clarity. I barely spoke as it slid out with the moments still dancing on the inside of my eyelids.

"Yes."

I bit my lip knowing I couldn't take my answer back. Knowing that one word would undo all that I just pleaded for. Knowing that it was selfish to lead him to believe something that once was. I don't know if I could be what I was before.

He didn't move for a second too long. My heavy eyes slowly opening, gliding up from his unbuttoned collar, to his parted lips and heavy breathing. Then too his smoldering heavy set gaze.

He stared down at me searching my soul for something I knew for sure didn't exist, even though he was sure it did.

"Then there is another answer to all of this." His voice dripping with his need for me.

Subconsciously I sighed knowing this wasn't the

reaction I wanted. I knew what he was going to say, and it had been one of the scenarios I thought hard about.

Gently, I started pulling my hands out of his. He was so close to me, I searched for something to focus on. Landing on the second button down from his collar. It was half through the hole waiting to be pushed or pulled through.

"There are two tickets. I want to go with you. Please let me be with you, I can't stand the idea of two weeks apart. I would follow you anywhere Vi. France, Australia, Russia, the moon, as long as I'm with you, I don't care."

"Max…."

I let out an exhausted sigh shaking my head.

"I…"

Before I could figure out what to say next, his lips were pleading with mine, my lips responding far too easily. His fierce kiss breathed light into dark places of my body that I didn't know existed. Deep and begging, he was done trying to convince me with his words. Everything blurred together. Me, Max, alone, apart, together, need, want. It melted into a humming yes from somewhere in the back of my mind. I knew there was no turning back, but my hunger for him forced its way up my spine and took over, body and soul. I knew Max, better than myself, and he was every comfort to me and truly all that I had left in the world. My strength evaporated, and all I could think about was how badly I wanted him. Even with that thought, I knew I wasn't good for him.

But he was the puppy I had to release, to be free and normal and happy.

Cutting that thought in two, he eagerly picked me up and set me on the counter top. I broke away from his lips and pulled back from him to look at his face in the dark lit room. He looked back at me while slowly rubbing my back where dress and flesh met. I realized then I wasn't going to make him stop, a piece of me wanted to, but I couldn't. I was done fighting him and this uncontrollable hunger for him inside me. Deep down I didn't want to, as selfish as that made me. I brought my hands up to his face, and pulled him to me. Our kiss caught fire, fast, and set ablaze into a wild craving of flesh.

A different kind of need and want, for desire and lust. For tonight, I knew I wanted to be his, and there was no mistaking my love and weakness of need in that.

His voice husky and deep, the hot air of his words brushing my lips.

"Wrap your legs around me Vi."

Without hesitation, I did as he said, and he immediately picked me up off the counter. Our lips pressed together, his barely leaving mine. He carried me past the kitchen, pressing me against the door to the master room, never getting enough of one another's lips.

Sliding the door open to the bedroom, I grazed down his smooth jaw line with my tongue and landed just above his collar bone. A moan escaping from his mouth, the breath of hot air tickling my ear. His hands grew firmer on me, carrying me into the dark room.

He sat down on the master bed, his grip not letting go of my position, setting me down on his lap. Our silent connection was thrumming loudly in my ears. He leaned back enough to push my tousled hair back from my face, and looked deeply at me. His eyes gave away what he was about to speak, his lips forming to say my name. I interrupted with my finger on his lips, rubbing my thumb back and forth on his bottom one.

Shaking my head I whispered, "No more talking."

I gathered my hair to one side, and pulled his hand from my rear, up to the zipper on the side of my dress. My body burning with every slow inch of his touch, unzipping down to my hip. He leaned in kissing the exposed flesh of my ribs while his hands slid my dress strap down my arm. Max took his time with his actions, stirring me with need.

Once one side was off, his light touch was on the other side slowly pushing down what remained of my dress. The delicate fabric fell away, along with anything else I held back from him. My shield was down, and I was fully exposed, showing what little of myself I had. Nothing can be put back in place that the force of nature hasn't already taken.

Max's hand rested on my hip, running his touch around my panty line. I looked into his eyes and saw a look I had never seen from him before. He wanted me, there is no other way to describe the intensity that was there. The trust and respect mixed with the deep understanding many years between each other collided with a need I could tell he was trying hard to control.

Meeting my stare, his hand drew a line of fire from my belly button, slowly up my chest, pushing me back slowly. I leaned back putting my weight on his thighs, letting my hair hang loosely behind me. His searing lips followed the sensitive trail his hand just forged, while his other hand spread over the small of my back pressing my waist to his. As his mouth slowly devoured the front of me, he pulled his hand up at my back slowly bringing my torso closer and closer to him. Nothing was clear in my mind any more, only that I didn't want him to stop.

His perfect lips brushed the skin at my collarbones, making my breathing falter. I slowly leaned up, being pulled toward him. My lips met his in a tangled craving that left me wanting more with every greedy one I took. My hands impatiently found the fastened belt at his waist, and freed it with an impatient pull, breaking the clasp without caring about being gentle.

Pulling back from him, his hands tightened on my hips, hoping I wasn't going to run I assume. I took my time unbuttoning his shirt starting with the teasing half pulled buttoned that gave me this choice earlier.

I ran my hands from his bare shoulders down his arms taking the shirt down with my slow movement. Once it was off, he gave me no time to return to his mouth before his was on mine. My hands explored his rigid upper body, to his abs, then around towards his back, pulling his body as close as I could to touch mine. Desperately trying to touch every inch of my skin to his.

A low, almost pained growl came from Max, catching in my mouth. I started to lessen my unsteady mouth from his thinking I had hurt him in some way, but his hand was at the nape of my neck pushing me, crashing my mouth into his and not letting go. His intensity for me melted everything into nothing but sensation. It was just he and I.

In a very carnal way, he lifted me like I was no challenge at all, and turned to lay me down on the bed. Slowly he released his grip on me, leaving me cool where his skin was just touching mine. With hesitation, he pulled further back, my body following his up to keep our bodies together. His hands came up and held my face, letting his mouth release mine, catching my bottom lip in his teeth. His mouth never leaving my body, slowly down my throat following the same trail his mouth was now familiar with. He pushed me down to the bed with his hand, gently letting me melt back down.

He worshipped my body with every abrupt move, and every languid one.

Putting his feet down to the floor and standing up straight, he slid my dress from my waist. Taking one foot out at a time and tossed it without breaking our fevered stare. With one hand he unbuttoned his black dress pants, and unzipped the zipper letting them fall to the floor. In a careless move, he tossed them in the same direction as the dress, building a pile of clothes in the corner.

I closed my eyes, trying hard not to stare and bring attention to the inexperience and slight awkwardness creeping up my spine.

The mattress dipping between my legs, Max kneeled with one knee between mine, and the other at the side of my thigh. His bare stomach pressed to mine igniting unknown fervor from deep down inside of me, causing my eyes to slowly open. I stared directly into his.

He mapped my body with his mouth, building me higher and higher with need. His lips brought me to places I had never seen, wanting him impatiently. As soon as my excitement started to peak, he'd bring me back down soothing me.

Painting and moaning, sinking into the duvet with anticipation and sweat, he slowly removed my black lace boy cut panties. He stood at the foot of the bed again, holding them in his hand, his eyes raking over my body with a look on his face that told me he loved everything he saw. His grey boxer briefs barely hugging his hips, my eyes couldn't help but wander. My breath caught at the full sight of how insanely sexy he is. At the same time I was checking him out, he groaned a deep heady growl, his eyes still on my nakedness on display in front of him.

"God, Vi…"

He knelt beside me, laying parallel to my body with his free hand roaming freely up my front, then up to my face where it stayed.

"You are so beautiful baby, every piece of you. I love your body. I've always loved your body, but now I can fully appreciate it. If I could touch your bare flesh forever, it wouldn't be enough."

Hooded eyes mirrored on both our faces, my mouth reached his in a slow and deep torturous kiss. I moaned, pushing my body sideways to his.

"Vi?" His breathing was heavy, pulling away from my mouth. I didn't answer, my hands searching for more of him to feel.

He held my torso with his whole arm, tightening me to him. Breathlessly sucking and kissing my neck up to my ear sending new feelings to every tip of my body.

Whispering next to my ear, then pulling up to measure my reaction, "Vi, is this your first time?"

My eyes flew open, looking into his not able to speak. Was it that obvious?

His voice was soft, his lips caressing my jawline waiting for an answer. His hand never stopped rubbing the small of my back knowing it would sooth the awkwardness snaking back up, this time more like a lightning strike than a subdued slither.

"Please tell me I'm your first Vi, I've been waiting for this for a very long time and I want all of you." His breath on my collar bone was making my body melt back into his.

His words undoing me more than when he undressed me. He knew me well, knowing I'd rather get up and run thinking I was being called out for being a virgin and having very little experience. Instead of waiting for my answer he laid all his cards out, telling me exactly what would turn me back to him, he wants to be my first.

"You are my first everything Max." My voice came out low and soft, giving away the vulnerability I felt.

Max's head shifted up to look at me, his eyes shifted from a hopeful glare to heated liquid chocolate as my words sunk in. A possessive smirk tugged at the corner of his lips, greedily taking my mouth to his. My body reacting, turning in further to be flush with his bare flesh.

My hands felt their way down until the band of his boxer briefs stopped my flesh on his. My thumbs dug into the band, pulling softly. Max gave me a squeeze then stood back on the floor pulling them down. He turned to a dresser directly behind him, pulling out a drawer. I heard the sound of a foil wrapper, and looked down at him, almost too dark to see his outline. He stood, staring admiringly at me completely naked. He could tell what I was awkwardly trying to avoid landing my gaze on, and was soon half on top of me, one leg between my thighs the other to my side again.

Feeling a pang of anxiety curdle with my want for Max, my body curved to his, craving his comfort to sooth it.

"I've wanted you for so long Vi." His forehead pressed against mine. "I love you so damn much, it's hard for me to tear my lips from yours. You're everything to me."

He leaned in and kissed me sweetly, showing me the softness of his feelings.

"I want you so bad, but if you aren't ready just say so.

I can feel you tense up with me mentioning it."

I shook my head, letting a single tear slip from my over stimulated emotions. I put both my hands on his face and retuned his gentle kiss, bringing it from his lips over his jaw to his ear, and hugged him.

His kisses took over my neck driving down further, sweeping me into an exotic erogenous tidal wave.

My mind was buried, checked out, and all that mattered was his mouth on mine and his hands on my body. They searched my body thoroughly from my over sensitive breasts down to the hollow of my pubic bone. His hand paused with a fierceness in his wanting kiss. His whole body wanted me, taking me in whatever way he pleased, always searching for my resistance. Not finding any. I trusted him with my life, with the sliver of a beating heart that I have, and with my being.

Slowly, sliding his touch down the inside of one of my thighs, he gently urged it open. My other caught under his inner thigh, pinning it to the bed. From my thigh his hand touched me in foreign ways, moaning possessively into my mouth as he continued his conquest over me. He was so gentle with every movement, but soundlessly commanding my body what he wanted from me, or what I wanted from him. It was all the same.

Building my body into a tense greedy need, his name rolling thoughtlessly on my exhaled breath. He pulled away, leaving my hands searching for his attention. My eyes closed, I heard a tearing of foil and a moment later he was kissing and tracing around my belly button with his tongue. My body naturally responding to his, my spine curved and my head pushed back into the bed with a hot and heavy sound passing over my lips.

Effortlessly, he positioned himself between my thighs. The blood coursing through my veins at light speed heightened my awareness on every square inch he was exposing himself to down there. Max's torso met mine again, relaxing any trepidation starting to build inside of me. His need screaming into my soul through his eyes, he kissed me slowly, building me to an eager feeding of emotions. His hand running down my ribs, hooking itself on the back of my knee, raising my leg up. Then slowly brought his touch downwards to my rear. My hips speaking an unknown language, angled to accept him.

Slowly, and reassuringly he eased into me. His guttural sounds and his whispered words intimately preaching his desire for me. He filled me with his admiration, his lust, his greed, and his craving. He consumed me with his gaze, showing my body how to be his, and showing my heart how I can never turn away from him. As he was ruined for anyone else, I was now forever his.

My soul letting go with a sensual rhythm that possessed me, no limitations. I gave him what I had and he took me from one side to the other in my heated surrender until we both were flying.

Our breathing rugged, Max rested his forehead to mine, our lungs searching for air. He kissed me sweetly and softly, pulling away. I caught his face in my hands, stopping him at arm's length. His demeanor completely serene, a look I had never seen written on his face before.

His hand reached up to mine, holding it in place. After a few seconds he smiled, the look of intimacy streaking his eyes, pulling my fingers to his mouth and kissing them tenderly. He stood, grabbing two quilts from the corner of the small room and laid back down beside me, guiding my worn out body sideways. Spooning me, he pulled both quilts over us. I shivered at their cool touch.

Murmuring in my ear, Max wrapped around me protectively, every physical way he could.

"I've always been yours Vi, always will be."

He turned my head with his finger on my chin and kissed me so softly I thought we were weightless.

His warmth enveloped me as I rested my head on his bicep. Immediately, I caved to my exhaustion. It lapping at my tired body with the rolling lull of the boat.

EPILOGUE

There was barely enough light in the sky to see where the wood planks of the wharf were from the boat. The sun was slowly making its way to the horizon.

The notification that went off from my back pocket made me jump. I was already on edge from leaving Max sleeping in the master room. Leaving him was the only way I would get to Paris alone, even if I did leave the remaining shards of my heart behind with him. He didn't understand before, he wasn't ever going to let me go now. Him being so protective over me might be alright long term, but right now I just needed to do this. For me.

I walked faster down the wooden path to the main road, checking my cell phone for messages.

Where are you sneaking off to?

I read it a second time, then looked around. Kendra honked her horn to get my attention down neat the pier at the Yacht Club.

Paris I guess. I'm in need of a ride to my house, will you be my taxi this morning?

I wanted to write 'and hurry', my nerves were shot with the idea of Max following me. I just didn't need to deal with his reaction right now.

A pang of regret twisted inside of me. I just couldn't do this with him right now, I feel too much or nothing. I need to be half way whole for me to be worthy of his love. It's just too much.

Of course! Is everything ok though, how was last night?
You stayed with Max in his Uncle's boat I assume ;) :P
Stay put, I'm driving around and will pick you up there.

I smirked, she is like the inquisition when she thinks
something is up.

I'm... ok, overwhelmed... Will walk to meet you up
the road.

I looked over my shoulder to the silhouette of the boat
I had just left behind. I laid beside a man who now has my
everything, which I know isn't enough for him. He pushed
and knew I could love him this way. My heart is able to
ache for him, but what I need is to not ache. To not want
something so badly it is physically painful. It almost broke
me to leave him there, but everything right now is
foreshadowed by the gaping hole torn out of me searching
for my family. Finding some form of closure was my only
hope, but I didn't know how long that'd take or if he'd
even want me back once he wakes and realizes I've left.

I hope I find what I need in France.

To my readers, thank you so much for buying Kiss
of Affliction.

I can't wait to share the next installment of the
Never Kissed series!

Follow Me
www.kristamacbeath.com
www.facebook.com/authormacbeath
Twitter: @AuthorMacBeath

www.ingramcontent.com/pod-product-compliance
Lightning Source LLC
Chambersburg PA
CBHW050032180626
46810CB00002B/687